MW01714164

# My Darcy Vibrates...

***A collection of Pride and Prejudice-inspired steamy short stories***

by

**ENID WILSON**

To

my online fans

**Enid Wilson** loves sexy romance. Her writing career began with a daily newspaper, writing educational advice for students. She then branched out into writing marketing materials and advertising copy.

Enid's novels, *Bargain with the Devil* has been ranked in the top 50 best-selling historical romances on Amazon USA, *Really Angelic* in the top 30 best-selling Regency romances on Amazon Canada, *My Darcy Mutates* in the top 21 romantic short stories on Amazon UK and *Fire and Cross* in the top 39 British mysteries on Amazon.

Enid loves to hear from her readers. You can contact her at enid.wilson28@yahoo.com.au or www.enidwilson.com

Cover design by Lavender C

First published 2011

MY DARCY VIBRATES © 2011 by Enid Wilson

Except for use in any review, the reproduction or utilisation of this work in whole or in part in any form is forbidden without the permission of Enid Wilson, PO BOX 1091, Eastwood NSW 2122, Australia, www.enidwilson.com

This book is sold subject to the condition that it shall not be lent, resold, hired out or otherwise circulated without the prior consent of the author. This condition is imposed on the subsequent purchaser.

## Table of Contents

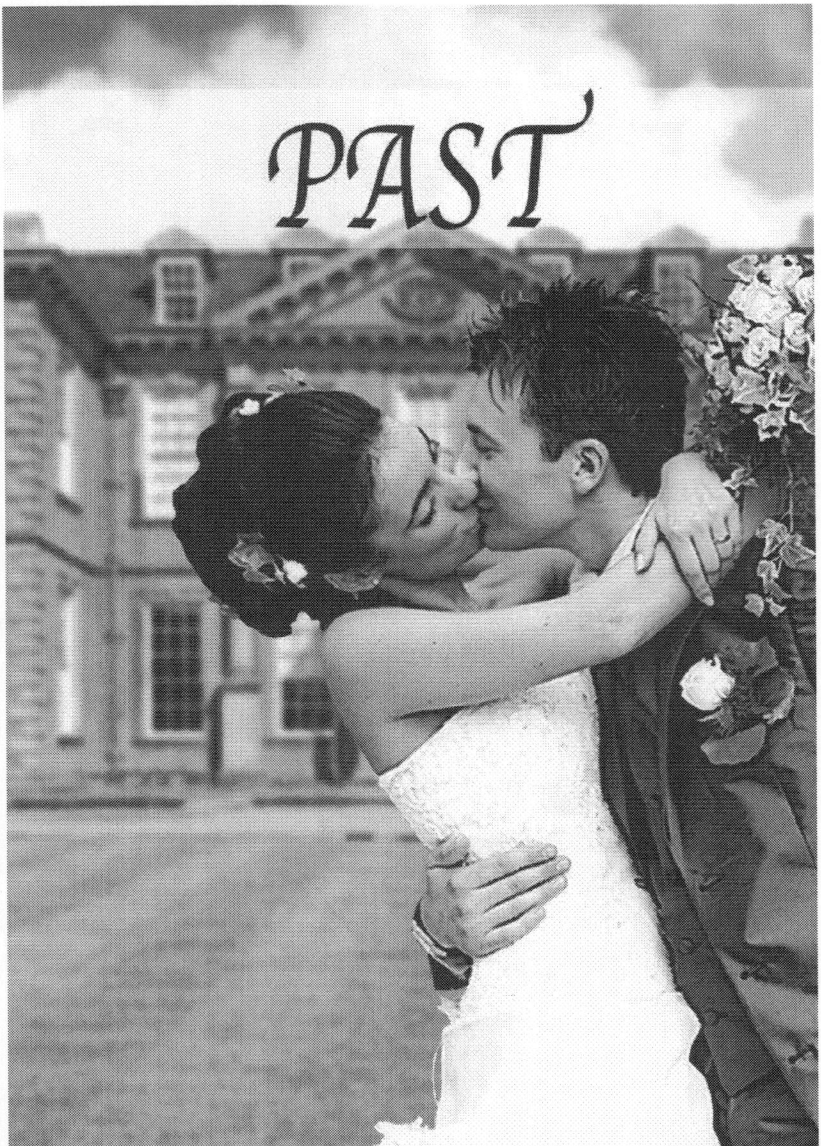
PAST

*What if Lizzy was rumoured to be in love with Wickham?*

## Out of Her Senses

*Every girl in or near Meryton was out of her senses about him for the first two months. - Pride and Prejudice - Chapter 47*

"Mrs. Long declared that the very mention of George Wickham's name drove every girl in or near Meryton out of her senses!" Mrs. Hurst exclaimed. Upon hearing the Bingley sisters' wicked laughter, Mr. Darcy's felt a shiver course down his spine.

Before he and his friend had announced their presence, they heard Mrs. Hurst's voice again.

"Did you not tell me, Caroline, that Miss Eliza was quite delighted with Mr. Wickham during the Netherfield Ball? I do wish she could hold off the stiff competition and snare him. Then your Mr. Darcy shall forget all about her fine eyes." Her cheers had the effect of turning the two men's faces bright red and their feet immobile.

Raising her voice in excitement, Miss Bingley concurred, “Well said! Perhaps Mr. Wickham could be most obliging and seduce Miss Jane Bennet as well. Then my lies about her not loving Charles would become a reality. I am sure, Mr. Darcy’s mousy little Georgiana will lift up Charles’s spirit once he hears that both the Miss Bennets have been compromised by the scoundrel.” Another round of indiscreet giggles could be heard coming from within the room.

Mr. Bingley took a big gulf of air and then dashed into the living room to confront his sisters, while Mr. Darcy walked out of Governor Square with fire in his eyes.

The latter was tormented by the possibility that Miss Elizabeth would have fallen under the spell of the scoundrel. What if she were to marry Wickham? The blackguard would bring her a lifetime of misery. Darcy could clearly see how her fine eyes would turn hollow; her once alluring and voluptuous body turn thin and bony; her wit and sparkle flatten.

*I could not bear it!* Darcy cried out loud, when he was finally alone in his study.

Not long afterwards, Mr. Bingley came to visit him.

“I have sent an express to open Netherfield Park,” an agitated Bingley said. “I know that tomorrow is Christmas Eve. But I am determined to pay the Bennets a call.”

“I have ordered the servants to pack for me already.” Darcy revealed. “I shall go with you.”

“Do not dream of interfering in my courtship with Jane!” Bingley rubbed his hands together, itching to punch his friend.

“I am going to ask for Mr. Bennet’s help to bring Wickham to justice.” Darcy’s face darkened.

“Then you are welcome to stay with me at Netherfield,” declared Bingley, finally calming down. “May I impose upon you for the night? My sisters sicken me. I cannot forebear breathing the same filthy air as them!"

Darcy poured a glass of his finest port for his friend and they stared at each other silently, each pondering their lovely ladies, until it was time to retire.

By midmorning, Longbourn greeted two haggard travellers. The eldest Miss Bennet looked pale on seeing Mr. Bingley. Elizabeth eyed the gentlemen with caution. The youngest Miss Bennets were nowhere to be seen. The Gardiner family who was spending the holiday with the Bennets looked at the newcomers with interest. Before Mrs. Bennet was given the opportunity to express her raptures on the gentlemen's visit, Darcy requested a meeting with Mr. Bennet.

Speechless, the Mistress of Longbourn could not fathom what Mr. Darcy business could be. Elizabeth recovered first. "Papa is in the library. I shall enquire after his availability."

"I...request to be present in the meeting too." Bingley added, as if it was an after thought. Mrs. Bennet grinned, hoping the meeting would be fortuitous for her eldest daughter.

Soon the two men were shown into the master's study.

"How may I help you?" Mr. Bennet graciously inquired of the flustered gentlemen.

Darcy looked at Bingley. The latter opened his mouth, but could not utter a word. Finally, Darcy drew in a deep breath, a sigh and then replied, "I would like to apologise for our sudden departure last month, without taking leave of you, sir."

Mr. Bennet's eyes turned from one gentleman to another. The corner of his lips curled up but he did not say anything, not indicating whether he accepted or declined the apology.

Mr. Darcy gathered himself again and continued. "We understand that Mr. Wickham has been a...charming addition to the neighbourhood. I would like you, sir, to know he is in fact a scoundrel. I do not wish to see Eli...your daughters hurt by the many falsehoods he spreads. I therefore requested this meeting to lay before you his connection with my family and his true nature."

Mr. Darcy proceeded to tell the older gentleman about the details of his father's will and his subsequent dealing with the blackguard, exhibiting the documents that showed the transactions of money. He did not reveal the Ramsgate incident but did show other paper indicating the support given by the Darcy family to some of the young women trifled with by Wickham.

By the time Darcy had finished, Mr. Bennet was in a rage about Mr. Wickham, a man he had thought of as charming before. Mr. Bennet agreed to gather information about any debts Wickham owed to local merchants and accompany the young men to see Colonel Forster after the Christmas.

"Before we go, sir," Mr. Bingley opened his mouth for the first time. "I would like to confess some deceit my sisters have imposed on Miss Bennet."

"Ah...my Jane has been rather dull, since November," Mr. Bennet poured himself a glass of wine. "I think her despondency began after she received a letter from Miss Bingley, saying that her brother admires Miss Darcy greatly."

Red haze burst through Bingley's face. But before he could reply, Darcy jumped in. "My sister is still very young."

"And I admire Jane a great deal more than Georgiana," Bingley cried out and turned to look at Darcy, either for encouragement or blessing. He quickly recovered. "Of course, what I meant to say is that Miss Darcy is like a little sister to me. But I have great admiration for Miss Bennet." He stumbled briefly, and then forged on, "and I would like to ask for your permission to court her."

"You want Mr. Darcy to give you permission to court his sister?" Mr. Bennet said with a wink, since Bingley had been staring at Darcy the whole time when he last spoke.

Bingley swung his head back to look at the older gentleman, "No, sir, Mr. Bennet, I am asking for your permission to court Jane, your eldest daughter, Miss Bennet."

"That is better," Mr. Bennet nodded. "At least your intention is now clearer."

"Then I have your permission, Sir?" The younger gentleman sprung up from his seat, leaned forward and moved as if to shake Mr. Bennet's hands.

"I did not say that." His words sent Bingley into a fit of anxiety. "I must ask Jane first. She may not consider someone who has shown himself to be so inconsistent of heart."

"Mr. Bennet, I promise I shall not listen to the lies of my sisters henceforth. I shall not listen to Darcy's dissuasion either. I shall beg Miss Bennet's forgiveness and love until she will have me. I am most determined to be constant to her, to stand by her side, for better or for worse, forever."

Darcy closed his eyes on hearing Bingley's declaration. Mr. Bennet clenched his jaw. "Mr. Darcy dissuaded you from courting my Jane?" He then turned to Mr. Darcy, "Sir, explain yourself, what fault did you find about us? Did you dismiss my girls because they have no dowry? No connections? Or no manners?" His voice raised a notch every time he moved closer to the tall gentleman.

Mr. Darcy held his hands behind his back. "I assure you, Sir, my objection to the match sprang from the best of intentions. I did not see that Miss Bennet's heart was touched by my friend. I did not want to see Bingley hurt."

"Yes, sir," Bingley added quickly. He did not want to see friction between his future father and his dear friend.

"Really, sir. Darcy here said he thought Miss Bennet demurely accepted my interest, but she did not seem to outwardly show any more significant feeling for me than she did for everyone else. It was entirely my fault. I was not confident enough to know her heart. I realize now that her smiles were indeed directed to me alone. My friend Darcy was only looking out for me. Miss Bennet was all that was proper in a lady, unlike the many cunning ladies of the town who only chased after me for my wealth."

Mr. Bennet's anger dissipated as quickly as it appeared. "My Jane is the model of gentility," he declared. She would not fawn over any man, no matter how rich. You can address Jane after I talk with her. But only if she is willing."

"Mr. Bennet," Darcy blurted out, "and I ask for your permission to court Miss Elizabeth."

"What?" Both Mr. Bennet and Bingley were surprised by Mr. Darcy's outburst.

"Yes, sir. I have admired Miss Elizabeth's quick wit, intelligence, vivacity and compassion since the beginning of our acquaintance."

"But Lizzy heard you say that she was not handsome enough to tempt you! Not for a mere dance!"

Mr. Darcy pulled at his neck cloth. He could not imagine a more torturous interview. "I regret the remark. When Bingley asked me to dance with Miss Elizabeth at the Meryton Assembly, I had hardly looked at her. But since then, I have been captivated by her fine eyes. Her manner is playful and her figure light and pleasing..." The glare from the older gentleman shut him up. It was not wise to mention his daughter's body. "It has been some time since I have considered Miss Elizabeth the handsomest woman of my acquaintance."

Mr. Bennet paced around the study, eyeing Mr. Darcy up and down for many minutes. The latter pulled at his tight cravat again. Finally, the master of Longbourn pulled open the door, "You stay here, Mr. Darcy. I shall ask Lizzy to come in. Mr. Bingley, I will talk to Jane. You can then talk to her out in the hothouse."

Bingley followed Mr. Bennet, a spring in his steps. Before he left the room, he turned to give Darcy a mock smack on the head.

Mr. Darcy returned with a fake kick on his friend's shin. His leg froze in mid air when Miss Elizabeth entered the room. The lady looked from one gentleman to another, surprised at their *boyish* display.

Bingley gave a hasty bow and closed the door while Darcy put his foot down and bowed deeply.

"Papa said you requested my presence," Elizabeth said with a frown.

"Yes, Miss Bennet. And did he explain..." Mr. Darcy sighed. Since the lady arrived so quickly, there would be no time for her father to explain about Mr. Wickham or the matter of courtship.

He launched into the explanation about his childhood friend first, careful to gauge her reaction. Her face turned from disbelief, to doubt, frustration and finally to anger. When he had finished, he asked, "I hope, Miss Bennet, you are not very disappointed at what I have told you."

"Disappointed?" Her voice was shaky.

"Mrs. Hurst had the impression from Mrs. Long that every girl in or near Meryton...was out of her senses about Wickham for the past month."

"Her intelligence was quite out of date, I am afraid. Mr. Wickham is engaged to Mary King, who has just inherited ten thousands pounds."

"So you are...not in love with him?" He asked eagerly.

"I do not see how that is any of your business, sir." She looked flustered.

He paced around the room, staring at her; sat on the chair, stood up and paced again. "Miss Bennet, I have asked for your father's permission to court you."

Elizabeth's eyes widened and she gasped for air. The confusion that passed over her features rendered her so adorable he was tempted to lean forward and kiss her soundly. But knowing that she had overhead him when they first met, he refrained. "I must apologise for the uncivil remark I made at the Meryton Assembly. I had not even looked at you properly when I made that comment. I only wished for Bingley to leave me alone. Since then, I have admired your beauty, listened to your witty conversation and worshipped your caring nature."

The tide of red spread from her face to her creamy ivory chest. Darcy felt a tightening in his trousers.

"I do not know...what to say," She murmured. His intense gaze made her hot and uncomfortable. "If I can be open with you..."

Mr. Darcy nodded and encouraged her to continue. "Even this morning, I had been thinking of Mr. Wickham as the most agreeable man I have ever met." Darcy wanted to protest. Her words were like cold water pouring onto his body, dousing his eagerness.

"And now, a few hours later, you have proved to me he is a scoundrel, a gambler and more. As for you, sir..."

"I have offended you," He hung his head.

"I should not be so vain. But I thought...you looked down on us, our society and separated Jane and Mr. Bingley. How could I feel amiable toward anyone like that?"

Mr. Darcy felt despondent. He wanted to shout out that he was a better person than she described, that he did not belittle Meryton's people and society nor did he separate...Ah but he did that. He should not have interfered with the courtship of his friend and her sister.

Charles was a grown man. Darcy had acted too much like the Bingley sisters when he was here a month ago.

Now he was given another chance. Overhearing the nasty conversations of the Bingley sisters gave him the courage to act on his instinct and return to Hertfordshire. And Elizabeth had shown her honesty and respectability. She did not fly to him with open arms, even though one of England's richest gentlemen was asking to court her. She wanted to be sure about his character. Anger left his body. He wanted to hold her tight and tell her he would learn and change his ways to gain her respect.

Instead of embracing her, he took her hands and declared in a deep and intense voice, "Miss Bennet, I am honoured that you see fit to reprimand me. I shall strive to be more gentlemanlike in future. I shall dance with every lady and converse with all the matrons in Meryton. And I shall keep my opinion about my friends to myself, if only you are willing to give me a chance."

Elizabeth squirmed on the chair. She could feel the heat of his body by the touch of his hands and smell his enticing manly aroma. His gaze held her eyes. She had never truly looked at him with such focus, not even during their dance at Netherfield. Now in close proximity, his eyes were pulling her to him. His lips were weaving magic on her senses. Would she really want him to court her? Could she see herself married to him? Her heart was beating madly. She wanted to say yes, to find out his true character, his intelligence and his passion. But she was also afraid of the consequences. What if she was wrong about him? What if, after getting to know him more she truly did not like him?

Biting her lips, she finally said in a quivering voice, "Will you allow me some time to think about this before I give you an answer?"

Disappointment clouded his face. But did he not promise that he would not act in an arrogant manner any more? This would be the time to show her that he could be patient and constant on such a matter as she requested. His thumbs rubbed her palm for a mere second. Then he released her hands and asked, "But will you still allow me to remain? To show you my true self?"

His eagerness was her undoing. She nodded and took the arm he offered. They left the study to join her family in the parlour.

"Mama, Mr. Darcy would like to join us for dinner." Elizabeth said.

***

Mr. Wickham was forced to leave the regiment due to his debt while Mr. Darcy began his 'courtship'. He accompanied Elizabeth to many social gatherings, big and small; throwing him in the company of her mother, youngest sisters, Mrs. Long, Mrs. Phillips and many more.

Mr. Bennet and Elizabeth never gave him the formal permission to court her but Darcy and Elizabeth had been seen together, conversing in excitement, dancing with intensity for many weeks. Everyone in Meryton assumed that they were in love.

***

Mr. Darcy's adulation in Meryton could never compare to the once charming Mr. Wickham's, for the former could never consciously charm like other young men. But there was one girl in Meryton who would often complain about him driving her out of her senses.

One day, inside the library at Netherfield, Mr. Darcy had locked the door and started kissing Elizabeth.

"Fitzwilliam! We should...not be doing this. What if someone comes in?" She breathed heavily.

"No one uses the library, except you and me," Standing behind her, he traced his lips along her earlobe, down her jaw and up to her lips. Through the smooth fabric of her dress, one of his hands reached around to fondle her creamy mound, rubbing and teasing her nipple; while another palmed her sex, and caressed her intimate folds.

"Please...Fitzwilliam," she panted.

"Please what, my Lizzy?"

"I want you."

"But we should not be doing this, you have just said." He moved his hands away from the sensitive parts of her body. She immediately moved them back to her scorching skin.

"I do not care. You are driving me out of my senses!" Pushing her hips backwards, she rubbed up against his arousal eagerly.

"I am mad for you too." Darcy breathed the words into her ears as his hands resumed worshipping her breasts and womanly folds.

Her moans and squirms urged him on. With frantic hands, he undid his breeches and drew up the hem of her dress. When his hot, hard manhood grazed along her folds, both of them let out a high pitched gasp.

"You...should not make so much noise," Elizabeth said as her body shook with anticipation.

But when he pushed his thick arousal into her warmth, stretching her inner muscles, she screamed out loud. Biting his lips, he had one hand inside her dress, squeezing her breast and another rubbing her folds as he impaled into her from behind. Thrust by thrust, stroke by stroke, he pushed her to higher and higher heights. She pressed her hands against the door, tilting up her buttocks to meet his pounding. Their sweat, their skin and their scent unified as one. When Darcy finally tipped her over edge, her scream was so ear-maddening that he was sure the whole of Meryton would have heard of it.

"I think it is you, Mrs. Darcy, who is stirring up all the furore!" He murmured as he rested his heated body against her.

Yes, Mr. Darcy and Elizabeth were married, several years before. But their senses often deserted them when their passion flared suddenly.

And why were they at Netherfield? Mr. Darcy bought it for Elizabeth as a wedding gift and for them to use when they visited Hertfordshire. After all, it was the place he first lost his senses and fell in love with her.

*What if Mr. Darcy was badmouthed by Wickham?*

## Who Should Be Jealous?

"I think Lizzy is jealous of me! That is why she was not interested in hearing anything about my wedding, at first."

Lydia Bennet's high pitch voice shattered Elizabeth's concentration. Elizabeth was sitting on a log, hidden from the views of others behind the large oak tree at the back of the garden. At Lydia's words, she rolled her eyes and tried to continue her reading, but she soon heard Lydia and someone settling onto the bench beneath the tree. She had just begun giving serious thought to finding an escape route when she heard Kitty asked, "But why would Lizzy be jealous of you?"

"Isn't it obvious? She was smitten with my handsome husband, once before. Of course she is jealous that it is I who caught Wickham, and not she!"

Elizabeth wanted to jump out and exclaim to Lydia that she was welcome to a hundred Wickhams, but Kitty sighed and said, "Yes, your husband is wonderfully handsome! I suppose he behaved much better than Papa on the wedding night."

Elizabeth's eyes popped open, and she nearly made a surprised sound that would have betrayed her presence. How could Kitty compare Papa with that rake Wickham? And how would she know anything about their parents' wedding night? Before she could protest, she heard Lydia's raucous chuckle.

"Oh, Kitty, I see that you remember what Mama told us a few months ago."

"How could I forget? Mama said that Papa was horrible on their wedding night. He caused her a great deal of pain, then fell into a slumber immediately afterward and snored loudly throughout the night. She said she only tolerated his attentions once in a while because she wanted to bear a son, so that she would not be thrown out of Longbourn if anything happened to Papa."

Elizabeth wanted to cover her ears and stopped listening to her silly sisters. Of course she knew that her mother often berated her father over matters great and small, simply because he would not give in to her every foolish wish. But she had never imagined that Mama would talk about Papa in such a vulgar manner to her own daughters.

"I think all men are like that." Lydia said.

"What! Even your handsome George? Did he hurt you a lot? "

"No...but I was a tiny bit disappointed."

"Why?"

"Before we eloped, he would spend ages kissing and fondling me. But on the night we eloped, he just did it quickly, lifted my gown, thrust into me once or twice, and then went to sleep."

Elizabeth blushed from head to toe. She covered her ears with her hands but found, to her distress, that she could still hear Lydia and Kitty's conversation.

"Was it painful?"

"Not really. He is not as large as he had claimed. He told me before that he was quite big! And he laughed and said that Mr. Darcy was this small." A burst of giggles was heard.

Elizabeth nearly dropped from the log upon which she was sitting. How had Mr. Darcy's body come into the conversation?! Had Wickham no shame! Not only did he spread lies about Mr. Darcy's character, he also laughed at Mr. Darcy's stature. Elizabeth suddenly felt very hot and flustered when she remembered THE dream.

***

She thought of it as THE dream because it was the most embarrassing and yet fascinating dream of her life.

It had come to her on the night after Elizabeth first met Mr. Darcy, who was dripping wet from his swim, at Pemberley. Upon Mrs. Reynolds's commendations, Elizabeth had for the first time developed a gentle sensation and a deeper sentiment towards Mr. Darcy. That night, she could not seem to get the image of Mr. Darcy out of her head.

He was wet from head to toe. His neck cloth and coat were nowhere to be seen. The top few buttons of his shirt were open, allowing Elizabeth a glimpse of his chest hair. The shirt's tail had pulled out from his breeches.

Mr. Darcy paced around the room. Suddenly he stopped in front of her and said, "You must allow me to tell you how ardently I admire and love you."

Dear god! She was back at Hunsford, but with a very wet Mr. Darcy proposing to her! Elizabeth thought about how seriously she had wrongly accused him and how Mrs. Reynolds had enlightened her about his truly admirable character. She wanted to relieve the pain she had caused him in Hunsford in April. So she worked up her courage and walked gingerly to stand in front of him. Slowly, she raised her right hand and touched his curly hair tenderly, then ran her fingertips slowly down to his cheek and said, "Thank you, Mr. Darcy. I admire you, as well."

His intense countenance changed immediately, and the most beautiful smile appeared on his face. He took a step forward, wrapped his arms around Elizabeth's waist, pressed his wet body to her and asked, "Would you make me the happiest man on earth and consent to be my wife?"

Elizabeth shivered. She could feel the dampness of her clothes and the heat that emanated from Mr. Darcy. Looking directly into his eyes, she replied, "Yes, Mr. Darcy. I would be most honoured to become your wife."

Mr. Darcy tightened his hold of her waist. They were now chest-to-chest in an embrace. After a few intense minutes at such close proximity, he moved to recline on the long settee and brought Elizabeth down onto his lap in the most scandalous position, straddling him.

Elizabeth's eyes widened. She could feel a solid bulge of hot flesh beneath the apex of her legs, and her nipples hardened under the damp muslin of her bodice. She squirmed and tried to stand, but Mr. Darcy held her tightly and whispered, "My dearest, loveliest Elizabeth, do not be afraid! I want to help you to feel comfortable with me. You are so small and I am so big... I do not want to frighten you on our wedding night, so I want you to know my body as soon as possible. In fact, I have been unable to stop thinking about it, ever since your stay at Netherfield in November."

"Insufferable man! How could you have such thoughts about me so early in our acquaintance?"

Mr. Darcy's smile turned to a grin, and he slid one hand under Elizabeth's bottom and loosened the buttons of his breeches. Suddenly Elizabeth felt something hard and long pressing through her dress, touching her secret place.

"Oh, Elizabeth! My thoughts were not rakish at all. They were, in fact, very lovely."

He proceeded to demonstrate just how lovely he could be by kissing her passionately. He reclined further down the settee, with her on top of him, her hands arranged on his chest. Trailing his lips along her creamy neck, he pushed the neckline of her gown down and kissed her breasts. He licked and suckled her nipples hungrily while his fingers found their way under the dress to pleasure her secret valley, where no man had ever touched her before.

Elizabeth threw back her head and arched her back, moaning loudly. She was close to reaching her peak when she felt Mr. Darcy slow the tempo. *Teasing man*, she thought. After a few more minutes of slow caresses, he grasped her by the waist and lifted her up slightly, then slowly lowered her onto his hard length, inch by inch.

He was big and she was tight. She felt the pain but she also sensed the pleasure. He saw her generous bosoms proudly protrude from her neckline, perfectly positioned for him to taste and fondle. He licked her breasts and suckled her nipples hard. When she was lost in the delightful sensations, he suddenly thrust hard, driving into her all the way. Then he stopped, as she cried out.

"Sorry, my dear," he panted, "but all will be good in a moment."

He held her hips and moved her, guiding her to ride him fiercely. They thrust into each other, on and on, until the afternoon sun dimmed. With one last mighty thrust and a loud moan from him, Elizabeth...banged her head against the settee and woke from her hot dream.

Elizabeth had never before had an erotic dream, and that one had been so vivid that she had trouble meeting Mr. Darcy's eyes, the next morning when he brought his sister to visit her in Lambton.

***

Kitty's loud laugh distracted Elizabeth from her steamy reverie and brought her back from Derbyshire to Longbourn.

"How funny that Mr. Darcy should be small!"

"Why are we talking about that dull Mr. Darcy?"

Elizabeth could not have agreed more. *Yes, why? And in such a scandalous way!*

"Because Maria told me that Charlotte thought Mr. Darcy was in love with Lizzy."

Elizabeth stopped breathing. *How could you, Charlotte!*

"What? Poor Lizzy! George says that Mr. Darcy does not like women much."

"How would he know?"

"Silly girl! They grew up together. George said that no woman could be happily married to Mr. Darcy, since he does not have the right equipment and hasn't practiced at all."

"But Lydia, you said you were not satisfied with George, either!"

"I didn't."

"Yes, you did."

"In fact I am very satisfied! I am married before my two so-called 'beautiful and intelligent' elder sisters. I caught myself a husband at sixteen, while they were still living at home like a pair of dry old plums. My husband is handsome and admired by everyone in Hertfordshire. The red coats in Brighton adore me. And I am sure everyone will love me in the North, as well. Indeed, I am the happiest woman in the world! I do not care what you think, Kitty! I am going back to the house for tea with my handsome George."

***

Elizabeth sat in front of the mirror and looked at herself. She was not a dry old plum but a beautiful, lively and intelligent woman who was adored by her new husband, Fitzwilliam, as she now called Mr. Darcy.

She knew she should not be nervous about what would happen in the next few minutes, because Aunt Magdalene has given her very good advice. Mrs. Gardiner said Mr. Darcy would be very gentle with her because he had deep affection for her. He would respect her wishes and make certain that she enjoyed the experience of the union.

Of course, Elizabeth's mother had given quite a different set of advice. Her mother opined that Mr. Darcy had probably selected her as his wife over a woman with position and wealth because he wanted a country wife that he could control.

"He is so rich, and has so much power in the church. He will be a brute in the marriage bed, I am certain. So, poor Lizzy, you will have to bear it all and not make him angry. But I think tall men are like fat men – they are clumsy and will not want to do much in bed. So do not worry, Lizzy, he shall not last a minute. Just close your eyes and think of all the carriages and beautiful gowns."

And then there was the ridiculous letter that she had received from Lydia, who had repeated in print what she had heard from that rake Wickham about Mr. Darcy not liking women, and so she was sending her condolences to Elizabeth.

Throughout their engagement, Elizabeth was, in fact, a bit concerned. Mr. Darcy never attempted to kiss her lips or embrace her. He seemed proper and serious all of the time. She knew that Mr. Bingley had stolen a few ardent kisses from Jane, and Elizabeth was quite envious of her on that account.

But then she told herself: *I do not care about this. It is just the physical side of a marriage. He is caring, honest, responsible and intelligent. And he loves me to pieces. How can I inspire such an emotion from such a great man? I am proud to be his wife and will be equally proud to be the mother of his children.*

With a renewed vow, Elizabeth marched towards her new husband's room and knocked on the door. It was opened immediately.

Mr. Darcy's neck cloth and coat were nowhere to be seen. The top few buttons of his shirt were open, showing Elizabeth a glimpse of black chest hair. The shirttail was pulled out from his breeches. Her eyes widened, and she thought: *Oh my god, he looks like the Fitzwilliam in THE dream, except that he is not wet.*

A grin broke out on his face, softening his often serious countenance and making him look quite boyish. He took Elizabeth by one hand and pulled her inside to sit down on the long settee in his room. *At least I am not on his lap yet*, Elizabeth thought, and blushed.

Mr. Darcy then held both of her hands in his, looked intently into her eyes, and said, "Lizzy, I love you."

"I love you, too, Fitzwilliam."

"I hope you have not felt frustrated with my behaviour during our engagement."

"Why would I be frustrated with you?" Lizzy was puzzled by the turn of their conversation.

"I know I am not like most men who are engaged to be married. I know that Cha.. I mean, I know that some men steal hot kisses and have intimate encounters with their fiancées. Some even anticipate their vows. But I did no such thing with you."

"Shocking! Did Mr. Bingley really share so much information about his courtship with you? I had better warn Jane that her husband has a big mouth. Did you reciprocate and share with him how we held our hands and played with each others' fingers beneath the table during dinners?"

"You know that I did no such thing. I do not like to gossip, least of all about the two of us. But there was a reason I was so proper during our engagement."

"Fitzwilliam, it is fine. You do not have to explain to me. I told you that I did not find your behaviour odd."

"Nevertheless, I did want to steal hot kisses from you – most desperately, in fact. And I dreamed of many...intimate encounters," he said with a bit of force, his expression growing flustered.

Elizabeth sensed a change in the atmosphere of the room, and she lowered her eyes to their joined hands and whispered, "Why did you not, then?" Was Mr. Darcy about to confess that he was deficient in his body and his skill, after all? How could she, a maiden, comfort him and help him to understand that she did not care about such things.

"Lizzy, I have thought about putting hot kisses all over your body, ever since your stay at Netherfield."

He moved suddenly nearer to Elizabeth. Startled, she lost her balance and tumbled down to recline on the settee, with him following. He did not press his upper body to her, though. His arms were braced on either side of her head, supporting his weight. But their lower bodies came into much closer proximity.

Elizabeth's eyes grew as big as saucers. This was turning out quite like her dream! She could not stop herself from asking, "Fitzwilliam! How could you have such ungentlemanly thoughts about me so early in our acquaintance?!"

“But I am a man, Lizzy! Your dresses have very low décolleté, and you have the most generous and enticing bosoms.”

He traced one hand around her décolleté, slowly pushing one side of it down to expose her pert, creamy breast.

“I wanted to kiss and suckle your breasts right there in the sitting room of Netherfield when you questioned my ideal of an accomplished lady. Did you not know that you were fast becoming my perfect woman then?”

He lowered his head and licked the creamy flesh of her exposed breast without touching her nipple. His hand moved to push the other side of the nightgown down. Using one finger, he rubbed her other nipple, enticing it with a circular motion.

Elizabeth squirmed and moaned beneath him. Never in her life had she received such a sensual assault, not even in her dream. She turned her head restlessly from side to side, then gasped when he finally closed his mouth over her nipple. He used his tongue to lave it, flick it and then suckle it like a hungry babe. His hand did not leave a moment idle, either, plucking hard at her other nipple. She felt hot lava cruise through her body and flow towards her womanhood.

Abruptly, Mr. Darcy pushed himself away from her.

“Do not stop, please,” Elizabeth begged.

“I am not going to stop. I just want to continue on the bed. There is not enough room here on the settee for me. You know I am big,” he said, and laughed.

Then he scooped her up in his arms, carried her over, and placed her on the bed, her breasts still exposed by the displaced neckline of her nightgown. She seemed to be viewing the room through a gentle haze, but she heard him say quite clearly that he was big. She wanted to ask him to clarify what he meant, but he lowered his lips to her, using his tongue to trace her upper lip while his hands continued to pleasure her breasts.

Elizabeth opened her mouth slightly, yielding to the force of his tongue. He triumphed with a muffled laugh and proceeded to slip his tongue into the inner sanctuary of her mouth, thrust it in and out in imitation of the ritual of mating.

At the same time, he seemed to have developed four hands to help him unfasten and push open her front-buttoned nightgown, while removing his own shirt and breeches in mere moments. While the tip of his tongue delved deeply enough to flirt with invading her throat, his hands shaped, squeezed, cupped and plucked at her breasts.

Elizabeth arched her back, offering herself, and felt two strong and muscular legs nudging her thighs apart.

Mr. Darcy's tongue left her mouth and began, instead, to caress her breasts while his long, clever fingers explored her womanhood. Her breathing quickened as she felt him place his large, hot, hard manhood against her, teasing her entrance. He slid it up and down at the apex of her legs with the expertise of a veteran rider, not yet trying to enter her at all.

Elizabeth sensed herself growing very wet and hot there, in response. She lacked the strength to raise her head and look, but she could feel him, and he was indeed extremely big. *Oh, my god! Does he truly believe that it will fit inside me? That Wickham is a lying rake!*

When Mr. Darcy slowed the sliding caress of his rod between her secret lips, she cried aloud, "Fitzwilliam, do not stop! Please. I need you."

She need not have feared, for he was not stopping. He was, in fact, adjusting his position to better advantage. His hands moved to the back of her right leg and raised it to his shoulder.

Elizabeth's whole body turned crimson, as she had never imagined being so nakedly exposed in front of another human being.

He then parted her private curls and began to press his manhood into her, slowly, inch by inch. To her astonishment and relief, her hot, wet flesh enveloped him. But then, abruptly, there was a barrier.

"Lizzy, it will hurt but I love you," he whispered into her ear, and then lowered his mouth to excite her breasts again. Elizabeth was lost in the sensation when she felt him thrust hard to break her maidenhead. She cried out, but it was not extremely painful, not least because he had distracted her with his kisses on her breasts. But it was such a strange sensation, to have him snuggled inside of her!

That was not all. He was still but halfway in. He continued to kiss her body as he pushed tenderly into her. When he was joined with her as closely as it was possible to be, he said, "My love, we are finally one!" Then he kissed away the sweat on her forehead and the tears on her face. "Are you ready to start this journey with me, Lizzy?"

Elizabeth's mind was scarcely functioning. She would have done anything for him, whatever he requested. She asked, "What journey?"

With a laugh, Mr. Darcy slowly pulled himself out almost fully and pressed into her again. "The journey of lovemaking, my dear."

He thrust in and out, on and on, until the candles by the bed burned out, and Elizabeth warmed from acceptance to eagerness to appetite, feeling her pulse quicken as her body began to rise to meet him of its own accord. Finally, aided by one last, mighty thrust from him, she reached her climax as he spilled his seed into her.

She was in heaven.

After she returned to earth, she felt Mr. Darcy caressing her tender breasts, then moving on to stroke her bottom and inner thighs.

"Well, Mrs. Darcy, are you satisfied with your new husband's performance?"

"Insufferable man!" Elizabeth exclaimed, and smacked his arm lightly.

"No more comment than that? In that case, I have to try a new strategy to pursue." He lowered his mouth toward Elizabeth's, but she turned aside, forestalling him. "But you have not finished telling why you were Mr. Proper before our wedding."

He sighed but indulged her curiosity. "I knew how you despised your youngest sister's infamous actions and elopement. And I knew that I would not be able to stop, once I started kissing you. I had so many heated dreams about you, after your stay at Netherfield, that I could not trust myself to resist taking you before our wedding. I dreamed of a new and different position or location for taking you to heaven nearly every night. And so, to be certain that I did not overstep, I stayed serious and proper all during our engagement. You do not know how I suffered!"

"Shocking, Fitzwilliam!" Elizabeth blushed from head to toe at this disclosure.

"But the good news is that I now have over three and hundred positions to sample with you," he said, and a very confident Mr. Darcy proceeded to demonstrate the second of those positions to his new wife.

*What if Elizabeth took a fall in Lambton?*

## A Tumble in Lambton

Elizabeth was reading the letters from Jane when she heard voices outside the parlour.

"Papa, looka 'ere, Mr Darcy's 'en th' stable ag'in. 'E mus be a-visitin' them folk from London!"

"Y'could be right, laddie. E's 'ere a'gin. Mus be that purty dark-'aired lady 'es a-wantin' t'court."

Elizabeth blushed. *Why is he here? I should go and change into a nicer dress. Oh, there is not enough time! Just pinch your cheeks, pull down the neckline and thrust your chest forward. Show more of your generous bosom. I am sure that is what Mama would say.*

"Miss? Mr. Darcy," the maid announced.

Darcy bowed and walked into the parlour.

"Miss Bennet."

"Mr. Darcy." *Look at those broad shoulders! The smooth-fitting, dark-green coat and the slightly dishevelled curly hair! Why have I never thought of him as handsome before? Lizzy, you have been blind as well as prejudiced where he is concerned.*

"Miss Bennet, I did not know that your aunt and uncle were not here. Otherwise, I would not have dreamed of intruding."

"My aunt and uncle are taking a walk by the church. I stayed behind to finish reading letters that I just received from Jane."

"I hope Miss Bennet and your family are all in good health."

*Don't start that 'family in good health' business again, sir. Just tell me why you are here!*

"I came... You see, I heard that, on the day your party visited Pemberley, you were unable to tour the entire grounds. I have come to invite your aunt, your uncle and you to take a carriage ride around the grounds this afternoon, before dinner."

"That is very kind of you, Mr. Darcy. But I am afraid that, after my aunt and uncle return from their morning walk, they will probably be too tired for another outing today."

"What a pity. The weather today is most agreeable."

*He looks disappointed. Maybe I should help him; otherwise he will just talk about the weather and then leave.*

"You are right about the weather. Indeed, now that I have finished Jane's letters, I would like to take a walk, too. Perhaps you could suggest where I might go?"

"May I show you some of the lovely sites in Lambton?"

"I would be honoured. Pray wait here for a few moments while I change."

*Where is my green morning dress? It is the thinnest and with the lowest cut! Let me tie the spencer more loosely. Then he can catch a glimpse of the upper part of the dress. Shame on you, Lizzy! You are employing the same arts and allurements as your scheming mother.*

Nevertheless, she loosened the spencer.

***

"Well, Miss Bennet, to the left of this road lies the church. To the right, it leads to the outlook. Which way would you prefer to go?"

"I would enjoy seeing the prospect at the outlook." *His arm is so strong and hard. And his scent! He has this musky wood smell. It is intoxicating. I wonder if he is going to renew his proposal. He sure looked very amorous yesterday when I defused the snide remark by that blasted Miss Bingley about Mr. Wickham. How can I leave him in no doubt about my feelings, as Charlotte previously advised...?*

Elizabeth was concentrating so hard on her determination to persuade Mr. Darcy to renew his proposal, that she was not watching where she was going. They were walking beside a gently sloping hill when she missed her footing. She yelped and tumbled sideways down the slope. Darcy was quick to wrap his arms around her, but the momentum of her fall carried him with her. They rolled for a few moments down the slope until they reached a level spot, with Mr. Darcy landing topmost.

"Elizabeth, are you hurt?" He cried out, with more concern than mere politeness strictly dictated. He used her first name without noticing, and was too shaken to think of removing his heavy body from hers.

Elizabeth's breath had been knocked out of her by the tumble. She gasped for air, and the rise and fall of her chest made her intensely conscious of Mr. Darcy's hard body stretched out upon the length of hers. She raised her head slightly, noting that the fall had caused her spencer to come altogether open. His broad, muscular torso was pressed against her breasts. The thin, low-cut dress offered little meaningful barrier. She could feel his muscles, and her nipples hardened immediately at the thought. She could also feel her face as it became hot and flushed. She closed her eyes, to savour this moment of forbidden closeness.

Mr. Darcy panicked upon seeing her eyes close. "Oh my god, Elizabeth, where are you hurt?" He moved his hands to feel her cheeks, neck, shoulders, chest and waist, searching for any possible injury.

*Oh, how I love the squeezing and fondling of his hands!* Elizabeth parted her lips, and a moan escaped her. As if of their own volition, her hands rose to splay across his back. She parted her legs slightly, allowing him to settle more thoroughly between her thighs.

He froze when he felt the touch of her hands on his back, and her thighs opening beneath him. He stared down at her facial expression, then lowered his gaze to her breasts. He could see that she was not in pain. *She is enjoying my ministration,* he realised with a thrill of surprise. *And her nipples! Even through her dress, I can see their rosy colour, and they feel quite firm and pert against my chest.*

"Oh, my dearest, loveliest Elizabeth!" He lowered his mouth and kissed her. When he felt her open her lips a little farther, welcoming him in, his passion surged. He slipped his tongue into her mouth, and allowed his hands to rove over her gorgeous breasts. When she did not recoil, he plucked her hardened nipples between his fingers. He could feel his arousal building, stretching his breeches. He rubbed his lower body against the apex of her thighs slowly to relieve the tightness.

Suddenly, the sound of birds flying overhead disturbed them, breaking the spell. Mr. Darcy rolled away from her, breathing deeply in an attempt to calm himself. After a few moments, he dared to look over at her.

She, too, was taking deep breaths. Her eyes were half closed, her lips swollen in the most appealing way, and her nipples were still clearly visible beneath the thin fabric of her bodice. In fact, the dress was little barrier to his penetrating gaze. He could see the undulating mounds and valleys of her body, and the sight was such a sweet one that it emboldened him.

"Elizabeth," he said softly, "my affections and wishes are unchanged from what they were last April. I still ardently admire and love you. Say that you will relieve my sufferings and consent to be my wife."

After a heart-stopping moment of silence that nearly slew him, she spoke. "Mr. Darcy," she said, "you are rather slow in your assessment. Did you realise that I did not chasten you when you addressed me more intimately by my Christian name? Have you not also noticed that I did not slap your face for taking liberties with my body? Were you unaware that I changed into the thinnest and lowest-cut of my dresses when I prepared to take this walk with you? I have been desperately using whatever arts and allurements I had at my disposal in an effort to gain your address, and I suspect that my mother would be very proud of me for doing so." She opened her eyes and arched her brow, gracing Mr. Darcy with a bright and teasing smile.

"Indeed, I noted all of those thing, and I do not mind your scheming in the least, so long as I am your sole target, my love. But tell me, was this tumble part of your strategy, as well?"

She coloured. "In truth, sir, the tumble was purely the work of providence! I was so distracted with my thoughts of how to induce you to renew your proposal that I did not properly watch where I stepped."

At that, they both began to laugh. Then Mr. Darcy lowered his head and kissed Elizabeth again, and they continued their tumble on the hill for quite some time.

***

"Papa, did 'yer see Mr Darcy 'an that dark-'aired lady? There clothes was all dirty wit' grass stains. Looks like thay musta taken a tumble, walkin' out."

"Yer could be right, laddie. Musta been a right serious tumble, at that!"

*What if Mr. Darcy followed Elizabeth during her ramble...*

## Three Rumbles for the Third Ramble

More than twice, in her ramble within the park, Elizabeth unexpectedly encountered Mr. Darcy. He never said a great deal but, on the occasion of their third rencontre, he seemed dead set against silence.

"Madam, you are an early riser."

"Sir, the same seems true of you, today."

"May I have the honour of accompanying you on your ramble?"

"As you wish."

"You have now been here for nearly two weeks. Do you find the estate and grounds to your liking?"

"I find the estate grand and luxuriantly furnished. The grounds are a bit on the formal side for my taste. I confess that I prefer untamed beauty to calculated displays of nature."

"Untamed beauty! I, too, find I am more enchanted by natural handsomeness than splendours which are a result of man-made enhancement." He turned his head to gaze at her. Some of her lovely curls escaped from the bonnet, framing the rosy cheeks and creamy skin. *How I long to caress her cheeks and lips!*

"Sir, you are very wise! Nature transcends time, while man-made wonders become dilapidated all too easily."

"Well said, madam!" He paused for a moment, then continued, "And tell me, pray, what prompts your love of solitary walks?"

A mischievous smile graced her face. "The reasons I favour of solitary walks are many. I lack the patience to wait for some lazy late-riser to accompany me. I have no energy to spare for rushing my strides to match some tall company. And I have no use for idle conversation. As a result, solitary walks suit me very well indeed."

Mr. Darcy frowned. *She does not enjoy my company?* "But there are many advantages in the company of two. Have you not observed the connubial felicity possible within a happy marriage?"

"I confess that the unions I observe have shown a different tendency."

"How so?"

"I see more couples who were only brought together because their passion was stronger than their virtue."

"Madam, I will have you known that passion is the food of love!" He turned and embraced her, pressing her body tightly to his, then kissed her with passion and conviction.

Elizabeth was taken unawares by both the invasion of his strong tongue into her mouth and the press of his hard muscles against her body. Sweet sensations cruised from her mouth to every parts of her body. She clung to his arms and yielded helplessly to his ardour.

After endless moments, she felt him lower her onto the grass.

"Sir! This is broad daylight in a public ground."

"Do not be alarmed! I have taken you to my childhood hideaway. This glen has long been my favourite secret haunt, and I have never come across anyone here before."

She looked around and noticed, for the first time, that they were in fact in a deeply secluded glen, far from the park where she had begun her rambling. She would had no idea that, in her reverie, she had become so sidetracked.

He pressed her onto the grass, unfasten her bonnet and began to do the same with her spencer.

"Mr. Darcy, we cannot do this! It is most improper. People will notice the state of my clothing when we return."

"I know all the secret passages in the buildings. I can bring you back to your bedchamber without anyone seeing you. And it cannot be improper for a man ardently in love to show his affection. Let me teach you the meaning of passion!"

He lowered his head to lave her earlobe, her cheek, her jaw. His hands busily eased the dress off her shoulders, exposing her creamy, ripe breasts. He rubbed her nipples with avid attention before lowering his mouth to suckle them in turn.

Elizabeth gasped, and a stream of warmth flew toward her womanhood. She squirmed and moaned out loud, and her hands moved to his head, where her fingers tore at his hair. She said in a breathless voice, "Ardently... in love? But you... said nothing of it...in our... last two rambles. I have...objections to this mode... of declaration."

"What is ..." Mr. Darcy drew her skirts up to her waist, and slipped his hand to caress the core of her womanhood, "wrong with my mode of declaration?" A wicked smile appeared on his face, and he said, "Little

Lizzy seems to welcome my fingers quite eagerly! Indeed, she expresses no objection at all."

Elizabeth thrashed her head from side to side. His fingers wreaked havoc upon her breasts and secret valley. But she was determined to chasten him. "Mr. Darcy, you have ...behaved in the most... rakish manner! You... lured me to this secluded location in order... to seduce me."

"Ah now, Madam, admit that you want this as much as I do!" He guided her hands to help him unbutton his breeches. Once his arousal was free, her fingers – displaying a will of their own – wrapped around it gingerly.

"You are enormous!"

"I have anticipated the pleasure of your body in this glen for many days, since I first found out about your solitary walks. Now that I am in a position to take pleasure in you, my member of course stands proud and tall." He parted her thighs.

"I am ..." she was rendered momentarily speechless when she felt him push his thick manhood against her entrance, "scandalised, Sir!" Then she cried out sharply as he pushed into her to the hilt in one firm thrust.

Mr. Darcy felt her inner muscles pulse against him, squeezing his shaft. After a few moments, he helped her to wrap her legs around his waist, then held onto her buttocks as he settled into a quickening rhythm. He thrust faster and faster, moving her bottom up and down to match his tempo.

Enraptured, he slammed and pounded into her, on and on. Her legs and womanhood squeezed him hard when he was buried deep in her. Then she arched her body up when he was withdrawing from her, clearly not wanting to lose the contact. Their fierce mating was fast and loud. After endless moments, they reached their climax at the same time. He spilled his seed into her as she tightened around his manhood, milking him dry. Their ecstatic moans were like the rumbles of thunder from a receding storm.

When they had both caught their breath, he asked, "My dear Mrs. Darcy, how do you like our first coupling in the wood of Matlock?"

"Fitzwilliam, you are incorrigible!"

"This is your punishment for accusing me of being a lazy late-riser who is too tall and engages in idle conversation. As we are estranged from Lady Catherine and cannot go to Rosings, I do not mind acting out all of my fantasies from last Easter with you here. I think Matlock is very similar in style to Rosings."

"You mean you had such scandalising thoughts about me when we were rambling in Rosings, last Easter?"

"Certainly. In fact, what just transpired here is only one of my fantasies from that time. Shall I show you my second one?" Gently, he turned her and posed her on the ground on her hands and knees. Wrapping one arm around her waist, he tilted her hips upward. Then he knelt between her parted legs and slowly slid into her from behind, while his hands caressing her breasts and the folds on her secret lips. This second coupling started slowly, but their rapturous rumbles became as loud as the last time when they finally reached their peaks.

After that second blissful union, they sprawled on the grass, watching the birds and little animals as they chatted about pleasant, unimportant things.

After a while, Mr. Darcy turned to his wife and asked, "Elizabeth, really, why did you love rambling more than riding?"

"I just never learned to ride well."

"Poor thing! You have missed out on so much joy in life. Would you allow me to teach you to ride?"

"That would probably be a good idea, as there are so many lovely locations I want to see in Derbyshire which are more easily reached by riding. But pray tell me, Sir, what is your track record in teaching individuals to ride? I cannot entrust myself to just anyone."

"You dare to question my impeccable horsemanship? Let me start the first lesson with you now, and you will soon see how very qualified I am."

"Now? You jest! There is no horse here."

He flashed a devilish grin, gripped her by the waist and pulled her on top on him.

"My dearest, loveliest Elizabeth, this is my third fantasy! I longed to teach you to ride on me. Now straighten your back, relax your thighs, and place your hands on my torso."

She was taken surprise by his move. However, during their five months of marriage, he had always been the initiator, both in and outside of the bedroom, and she had gradually lost her inhibitions. He had taught her many new techniques and positions, since their wedding night, but she had never been the one who controlled their lovemaking.

She obeyed his instructions now without protesting. When she had done so, he moved his hands to pleasure her breasts and other parts of her body, quickly rendering her breathless. When she was hot and wet from his fondling, he urged her to lower herself onto his aroused shaft.

She moved slowly, taking him in, using the strength of her thighs and inner muscles to control the pace. The new position gave her an unspeakably fresh sensation. She anchored her hands on his hard torso and then used her thighs to lift and lower her body to ride this big horse, on and on, again and again.

Mr. Darcy held onto her small waist and helped her establish the rhythm. From time to time, his hands strayed to pluck her nipples, cup her jutting breasts and caress her womanhood.

It was not long before her eyes half-closed and her head thrashed with her movements. Both Elizabeth and Darcy moaned louder and louder and reached their climax with a rumbling scream.

"My sweet Elizabeth, how I enjoyed our third ramble! I got to act out all three of my fantasies in one go."

Future

*What if Mr. Darcy had certain urges?*

## Love, Suck and Sex

Once upon a time, vampires roamed the streets and sucked the blood out of men and women. The two greatest clans of vampires came from Derbyshire and Kent. Their thirst for blood turned into an unofficial contest. As a result, the human race was nearly wiped out by their rivalry until, one day, a temporary truce was reached. After that, the human population began to increase again, through mixed marriages with vampires and through cloning.

The bloodthirsty creatures were also castrated and cloned to become *suckones*. They no longer drank blood; instead, they nursed for pleasure, in the Annual Sucking Competition, when the electronic halo which suppressed their urges was released. Or, if they were lucky and found a partner upon whom they could feed their urges, they could wear the halo less frequently, thereby increasing their life expectancy.

Suckones sponsored less wealthy planets to provide partners for their competitors. Men and women participated in the week-long festival, and team members were tagged with bio-devices to monitor their pleasure levels. The couple who scored top marks would win and split the prize money.

"Commander Matlock, Spaceship Derbyshire will arrive on schedule at Planet Hertfordshire at 1800 hours," Colonel Richard Fitzwilliam reported.

"Good! And the position of SK?" Commander Andrew Matlock inquired.

"Spaceship Kent is at 69x 88y 33z, Sir! About 0.05 light years away."

"Wonderful! We'll arrive ahead of SK and have the highly advantageous opportunity of choosing first."

"Should I send the protocol signal to Hertfordshire now, Sir?"

"Yes."

However, after meeting teams from Goulding House, Purvis Lodge and Lucas Lodge, Matlock shook his head. He was in despair of finding the right partners for his team.

"The next one of decent size is Longbourn, Sir!" Richard announced, reading the data on his s-pad.

"Put the Commander of Longbourn on."

After a few seconds, a middle-aged woman with handsome features appeared on the s-screen.

"You're the Commander, madam?" Matlock was a bit unsure. She wore a rather silly uniform in red and pink, not at all like a commander with entrants for a serious competition.

"Indeed, Sir! I am Mrs. Bennet. My husband passed away, last year, and this will be the first time that Longbourn is participating in the Annual Sucking Competition. With generous funding from the suckones, I have been training my girls rigorously."

Matlock's eyes brightened. He had not anticipated finding such a gem in a backwater like Planet

Hertfordshire. First-time team partners always incited his suckone clan to perform. "I have three competitors, this time. Colonel Fitzwilliam, my son, has fifteen years of experience. He specialises in toe indulgence. William Darcy, my nephew, is a first-time participant, and prefers to keep his specialty confidential. Charles Bingley has three years experience, and he specialises in lip worship."

"Marvellous! I have five girls. All of them are, of course, first-time participants. Come, girls! This is Jane, Lydia, Kitty and Mary. Where is Lizzy? That wild girl. I only train my girls to give men pleasure. They have worked with silicon men, this past year, spending up to six hours a day in training."

Matlock looked at his team. Both Bingley and Richard had their eyes fixed on Jane. Darcy looked distant and uninterested. *Well, two out of three wasn't bad.* "Mrs. Bennet, expect us at 1824."

"You do us great honour, Commander Matlock!" Mrs. Bennet exclaimed, hugging and laughing with Lydia and Kitty.

Richard switched off the communication and said, "Jane Bennet is exceptionally pretty."

"She smiles too much," Darcy said. "Perhaps this Lizzy Bennet will be too plain to incite our pleasure. That may be why she is hiding."

"You amaze me, Darcy. All of the Bennet ladies are very pretty. And this Jane is angelic!" Bingley argued. "May I partner with her?"

"But I had my eyes on her first!" Richard said.

Matlock jumped in. "Richard, you know the rule. The least experienced suckones have first choice. So Darcy first, then Bingley, and you as the last."

"Bloody unfair rule!" Richard swore.

"Not at all," Matlock said. "First-timers need someone who can incite them to perform best. You are so experienced that you probably can perform at a reasonable level, even without your partner's stimulation."

"I know. It's just a bloody annoying rule!" Richard said again.

"You won't be in my way?" Bingley turned to ask Darcy.

"Go for her," Darcy replied. He might have to settle for the next beauty, Kitty Bennet, but she didn't look intelligent. It could be quite a bore to spend a whole week with her. If it weren't for his sister Georgiana, he wouldn't have entered this year's competition. She had urged him to get married, to find the right partner who could make his life more balanced. Now he regretted entering. They had been to over twenty sponsored planets, but no available woman seemed to stir his urges. In fact, he wasn't at all sure whether he had just one urge or whether he might have more, since his electronic halo had been fitted very young because of his exceptionally high hormone level. That was why he had asked Uncle Matlock not to talk about his urges to prospective partners.

A few minutes later, Spaceship Derbyshire docked at Longbourn. By this time, Mrs. Bennet had all five of her daughters in the receiving line. Darcy felt the eyes of Lizzy Bennet on him, the minute he walked down the plank. Her eyes sparkled with fire. Her mouth was closed in a thin line, and she had folded her arms across her chest, while she gave him a death glare.

*What did I do to earn such a reception?* Darcy wondered. But his eyes were drawn to her chest. He could see that she had the nicest pair of breasts he had encountered so far. Suddenly, he felt the urge to drink her essence attacking him. He raised his hand to touch the halo. It was comforting to know that it was firmly in place; otherwise, he might have torn open the green body suit worn by this Lizzy and started suckling her nipples in front of everyone.

"Welcome to Longbourn, Commander Matlock," Mrs. Bennet said cheerfully. "You have met all of my girls except Elizabeth."

Elizabeth gave the men a nod, her gaze still fixed on Darcy.

"Let's go in and have some tea," Mrs. Bennet said.

The visitors agreed. As Darcy turned to follow his uncle, Richard pulled him aside. "I want to partner with this Elizabeth. She looks hot."

"Sorry, Richard. I get to choose first, and she stirs my urges," Darcy said honestly. After meeting her, there was no way he could settle for any of her sisters.

"Bloody! I'm always left with the less attractive ones."

"Fifteen less attractive ones, compared to my one?"

"True, there have been some great beauties over the past years, but I haven't wanted to tie myself to any of them, yet." Richard clapped his cousin's shoulders. "Okay, let's go and get the competition going. I'll partner with Kitty. We may beat Kent, this time, with lacklustre like competitors Collins, Anne and Wickham on their team."

During tea, Richard sat next to Elizabeth and chatted with her. They laughed and debated animatedly. Darcy sat at the other end of the room, observing them with curious interest.

Once the tea was over, Matlock got down to business. "Darcy, as a first-timer, will start the choosing."

Darcy stood up and bowed to Mrs. Bennet. "I will partner with Miss Elizabeth Bennet."

The women were surprised, especially Lizzy herself. "I thought you said I was perhaps too plain to incite your interest?" she blurted out.

The men looked at each other. "Oh, didn't I shut down the communication channel properly?" Richard asked.

"We heard both you and Mr. Bingley state that you wanted to partner with Jane," Lydia said to Richard, with a pout.

Now Darcy understood why Elizabeth had been glaring at him, all this time. Her fiery response sparked his urges further. He walked purposefully toward her and gave her a bow, before picking her up and throwing her over his shoulder. "Uncle, I will go to Austen Arena now." He then touched the s-watch on his wrist, beaming Elizabeth and himself to the competition area underground on a planet in outer space.

"Put me down!" Elizabeth beat his back with her fists. "There's no need for such caveman tactics. I can walk!"

Darcy felt his urge increasing in exponential intensity. He looked at the various doors in the underground passage and quickly selected Eden Garden. Then, once he pushed the door shut, he put her down. They were scanned, and electronic monitors were tagged onto their ankles.

"I'm sorry about the speculations you overheard," he apologized. "Remember that I had not seen you, at that time. May I take off my halo now?"

"You didn't even bother to speak one word with me, back at the house, and you want to get right into the competition? Are you that desperate for the prize money?" She gave him another glare before walking farther into Eden and sitting down on a bench there, amid a field of wild lavender.

Darcy drew a deep breath to calm his urges. He walked toward her and explained, "You stirred my urges. I didn't dare to come too close you, at the house, in case I'd feel compelled to start worshiping you right in front of everyone."

She looked up at him with bright eyes. She tipped her head to the side, assessing him. "What are your urges?"

"Your beautiful breasts." He knelt down before her and slipped his arms around her waist. Her eyes widened and her spine straightened, which pushed her chest closer to him. Bowing his head, he started suckling her nipples through her body suit.

Even through the thick fabric, Elizabeth could feel his talented tongue playing with her nipples. She hadn't expected this handsome man to partner her. In fact, she had supposed that she would be asked to partner with Colonel Fitzwilliam, and therefore had imagined that her toes would be for expert treatment, instead.

But now, instead, this broody William Darcy was giving indescribable pleasure, even with his halo on. She couldn't imagine how the week would end. Could she forgive his arrogant remarks? But she couldn't think coherently anymore. His sucking was her undoing. Closing her eyes, she let her head loll back, pushing her breasts even farther toward him. Her skin and body tingled, and she could feel wetness gathering between her legs. Her hands tore at his hair helplessly.

It didn't take long for her to reach her first-ever climax. When she collapsed limply on the bench, he stood, picked her up, and carried her deeper into Eden, until he came to a pond by a gentle waterfall.

Lowering her to the ground by the pond's edge, he unzipped her body suit.

Elizabeth opened her eyes and looked at him.

"May I take off the halo?" Darcy requested again, his voice shaking with need.

She bit her lip and took pity on him. After all, it was just for the competition. "Let me," she said, and raised her hands.

He lowered his head and allowed her to unhook the halo and remove it.

Once it was off, he could no longer suppress his urges. His hands cupped and squeezed her pert breasts, shaping them to peaks as his tongue licked and laved her nipples until they hardened into rocks. He started sucking them, lightly at first, then harder and harder, for what seemed like an eternity. Elizabeth found herself pushed from one climax to another.

After almost an hour of intense activity, Darcy finally stopped and asked for permission to further undress her.

Her already crimson face turned further red. "My breasts are already bare. Why do you want me nude?"

"I want to see if I have other urges..." His gaze ran down her body, and he found himself increasingly convinced that he wanted to suck her pussy.

"All right...but only if you take off your body suit, too. I want to see you, as well," she challenged. "Otherwise, it wouldn't be fair."

He complied readily. The body suit had already been constraining his arousal for too long.

When he had cast the suit aside, he realised that Elizabeth was staring at him with an expression of surprise. "You look quite different from the silicon inflatable," she commented.

"In what way?"

"You're...larger." Her hands touched his shaft involuntarily. "Oh, and you're hot and velvety, not rubbery at all!"

Darcy sucked in a deep breath as, without asking for permission, she lowered her head and began to suck his cock. His aroused manhood grew larger still, filling her mouth. She used her tongue to stroke his skin, then sucked hard.

He grabbed the grass tight and thrust his hips up and down. Her tongue, lips and mouth were so well trained that it didn't take her long to push him over the edge. He groaned aloud and trembled in ecstasy for a long time.

"Did you like it?" Elizabeth asked when he finally lay still.

He wiped the sweat from his brows and pulled her to lie on top of him. "I can't even describe the pleasure. You suck so well! Do you have suckones' genes?"

"Not as far as we know. But my sisters and I spent hours learning how, over this past year. It would be a shame if I couldn't give you pleasure."

He looked at her fine eyes and felt himself truly connect with her. Pushing her body suit down eagerly, he allowed his hands to explore her mountains and valleys.

"May I have sex with you?" he asked.

"Why do you want to? We don't need to do that to win the competition."

"I want to be inside you when I suckle your nipples. The pleasure will double, I'm sure." The intensity of his eyes and voice gave her shivers. She nodded her permission.

He turned to lie on top of her and started the sucking ritual of her lovely full breasts again. No inch of areole, skin or muscle was left unexplored. When she reached a new climax, he pushed his thick cock into her hot and wet pussy. He was big, firm and impressive, invading her virgin core with hard, fast thrusts. She moaned, her hands digging into his back as he pounded into her again and again while continuing to suckle her nipples. Waves of intense pleasure attacked her body until he reached his peak, as well, and they tasted heaven together.

Darcy and Elizabeth spent a week of incredible time together, getting to know each other. He confirmed that he didn't just have urges to worship her nipples, but her pussy, too. By the time the competition ended, he had persuaded her to visit him on Pemberley, his planet. And it didn't take him long, thereafter, to convince her to marry him and help him relieve his urges for the rest of his long life.

And, of course, Team Derbyshire won that year's competition, with record-breaking scores.

*What if Mr. Darcy was an immortal?*

## Having My Baby – Again

Driving into the heavy fog, I was relieved to spot light coming from a run-down farm house. As I drew closer, however, I noticed that the light was flickering in the oddest way.

I didn't give it a second thought, but suddenly a wisp of black shadow crossed the road.

My eyes widened. *Was that a cat – or a man?*

I stepped hard on the brake, not wanting to hit whatever was out there. The car skidded on the slippery road, and I grabbed the wheel tight.

*Damn!*

The car swirled farther, grazed a tree and, with a bump and a squeak, came to a sudden stop.

I breathed a sigh of relief. At least it hadn't crash.

Shaking, I opened the door and inspected the car. The left front bumper was trashed, and the tire was totally flat.

*Now what?*

I took out my mobile, intending to call for roadside service...but there was no signal.

Damn my luck.

I grabbed my bag, wishing that I had brought my jacket. It was Halloween, and I was wearing a witch's costume that consisted of an extremely short garter skirt with moon and star appliqués, a bustier, a shrug and a hat. Sexy fishnets covered the length of my thighs, but they did not provide any warmth.

I walked at a brisk pace towards the old farm house. The fog was still heavy, the air damp, moist and cold. As I came nearer, I saw that the lights were indeed switching on and off in a peculiar way.

I stopped and looked at the farm house with concentration. The windows were dark, and each flicker of the lights looked like a number.

5, 17, 15, 7, 22, 17, 15, 7, 15, 27, 14, 11, 28, 28, 27

After several minutes of staring, I still couldn't understand what it was all about. All I knew for sure was that I was cold, so I continued to walk on, hoping to find help.

When I reached the door, I could see that it was a magnificent old house, as if the three-story structure had been designed and constructed with an artist's touch. It stood tall, and I imagined that the rooms inside must have high ceilings.

I ran my hand over the stunning wooden door and found a word carved there: *Pemberley*! What a lovely name.

I used the old-fashioned door knocker. It clinked against its metal strikeplate, and the sound echoed in the quiet night.

Although I waited, no one came to the door. But surely, with the lights on, there must be someone at home. I called out, "Hello? Is anyone here?"

Getting no answer, I walked along the wrap-around porch until I came to a huge room on the ground level, with floor to ceiling windows. I pressed my face nearer to the glass, trying to see in, and it was at that moment I saw a reflection above my face, right next to my witch's hat. It was the face of a tall man with ugly red scars, as if he had been burnt by the fires of hell. He raised his hand, looking for all the world like a devil.

I screamed and fainted.

***

When I awoke again, I found two pairs of eyes watching me anxiously. I had been placed on a bed, and music was audible, emanating from some distant room.

"Richard Fitzwilliam here. Sorry that Darcy gave you a scare." A middle-aged man with short blond hair smiled and offered a glass of water to me.

I sat up, had a sip and put the glass down on the bedside table. "I'm Elizabeth Bennet. My car has a flat tire." I looked at the other man curiously. He was tall, dark and very handsome, but he was wearing a fearsome frown.

"William Darcy. Sorry about what just happened," he mumbled, then moved away to stand in front of the window.

"Come along, Darcy. Apologise properly. You nearly caused this lady to have a heart attack."

Mr. Darcy turned back and tilted his head silently at Richard.

"Excuse me," Richard said, turning back to me. "I need to see to our guests. We're having a Halloween party. Will you stay?"

"I was on my way to a party, too," I confided. "My friends will be worried about me."

"I'm sorry, but I don't think we can fix your car tonight. Perhaps you would like to ring your friends and tell them you are at another party. You'll enjoy it." With that, Richard gave me a wink and another smile, then left the room.

I wanted to call after him, begging him not to leave me alone with this 'Darcy'.

As soon as we were alone together, Mr. Darcy came to kneel in front of me, took my hand and, to my astonishment, raised it to his lips.

I felt a shiver race down my spine. His lips were hot, and his gaze seemed to burn my skin. I wanted to pull my hand away, but he held it tightly.

"I really am sorry about what happened, just now. I was wearing a Halloween mask when you saw me." His expression grew even more intense. "But you came, my Lizzy!"

I blinked, startled. "How do you know my nickname?"

He raised his other hand and traced it along my cheek.

"It's always like that. I just need to signal my demand to nature, during Halloween," he whispered.

"Signal your demand? What are you talking about? What's always like *what*?" I demanded, thoroughly unsettled and confused.

"You saw the lights," he said simply.

"What does that have to do with anything?"

"Did you not understand the message?"

I shook my head.

He leaned closer and captured my lips with a tender kiss. When I tried to protest, he deepened it. His wet lips pried mine open and he thrust his tongue into my mouth.

His strong muscle probed and pushed. I felt the blood rushing through my body, and my resistance softened. As he sucked my tongue with such a vortex of force, an image formed in my mind.

It was Mr. Darcy...and me! He was sporting a cravat, waistcoat and breeches, while I wore an empire dress with a daring neckline. He was kissing me passionately, and one of his hands was caressing my swollen belly.

The kiss ended, and the vision faded. Shaken to my core, I looked into his eyes.

"You saw it, too?" he asked softly.

I nodded. "Us?" I queried, my eyes widened.

"Yes. You were having my baby."

I gasped, and he lowered his head to kiss me again.

A new picture came into my mind. This time, he was wearing a British army uniform. We seemed to be in the 1940s, and I was once again pregnant. Our kiss was as scorching as the last and the present.

Mr. Darcy raised his head and said with a smug smile, "You were having my baby again."

With that, he smoothed his hand along my shoulder and kissed the tender skin on my neck.

What more can I say? After that night, we did end up getting married, although not until we had weathered some huge fights about his arrogant interference with my sister Jane and a certain man called Wickham.

But yes, Mr. Darcy and his Lizzy still ended up together, no matter the time.

Oh, and did you understand Mr. Darcy's message?

*The message is 'Come to me, my Lizzy'.*

*What if Mr. Darcy's dead parents intervened?*

## Return from the Dead

Three days before Halloween, Darcy was working late at the office when a sudden storm broke out. Lightning pierced the dark sky, and loud thunder disturbed the quiet rooms. Not much later, all the lights were gone, and his computer shut down. When the lights came back on in a few minutes, he saw that his computer screen was still black. Then, out of the blue, white text scrolled across the black screen.

g d o h t l o p t h t e x h b a f l l j o n w r e v z e d n p h a l r t y y p o t x u b w f i j l l f n i r n d y v o z d u h r d l e p s t t i x n y t h b e f r j e n

As the printer switched on and began printing out the text, he heard a familiar female voice coming from the speakers of the computer. "Fitzwilliam, these are instructions from your late mother. Carry them out or risk punishment from the other world. This recording will destroy itself in ten seconds." Then a male voice was heard. "And from your father, as well. Don't be afraid, my boy. Just do as your mother said. I'm sure you are smart enough to decipher the message."

Darcy's eyes widened, and he jumped away from the computer. *Bloody hell! Did Richard plant this prank? I'm going to kill him! Where did he get Mother's and Father's voices, and how did he doctor them into this recording?*

The huge, empty office gave him an eerie feeling. Snatching up his jacket and brief case – and then, after a moment's reflection, the printout – he left the office.

He rang Richard, his cousin, repeatedly during his drive back to Pemberley, but Richard's mobile phone was switched off. Reaching home, Darcy paced around his study, glowering at the printout for hours, pondering how to decipher the message.

The phone finally rang, but it wasn't Richard. Instead, Bingley was on the line, inviting him to a masked Halloween party. Normally, he would not have agreed to go to such a function, since he hated dressing up in costume and socializing. Tonight, however, anything that could take his mind away from the recording and the bewildering printout was welcome. And so, after making Bingley swear that he would not disclose Darcy's choice of costume to Caroline, he agreed.

***

Darcy continued to call Richard over the next two days but failed to reach him.

Bingley sent the costume to him by courier, the day before the party. Darcy liked the mask. It covered his whole head, including his hair. Only his eyes and mouth were visible – a mouth that was now adorned by caps on his incisors, lending his teeth the look of a vampire.

As he drove his tinted silver blue Bentley Continental GTC to Bingley's house in costume, he felt truly like the Count, free to roam the earth in darkness.

The first person he encountered when he arrived was Caroline Bingley. He felt a thread of panic, and nearly turned back, but she didn't give him a second look in her busy quest to find him. She was dressed in a Hawaiian dance costume that showed off her self-proclaimed 'perfect' body. Her mask was tiny, leaving Darcy in no doubt as to whom she was.

Bingley didn't speak to him, just nodded to acknowledge his arrival. The party was in full swing. Darcy felt truly happy because he could move freely without anyone recognising him. No women fawned upon him, as there were six or seven different Draculas of similar height, in different colours. He was the black one. It had to be Bingley's doing, to provide some decoys for him, to help prevent Caroline from guessing his identity.

He had the luxury of savouring the food and wine and observing people, whether on the dance floor, in the dining room or out in the garden. A few hours into the party, he dropped his empty wine glass by accident, so he carried the broken glass into the kitchen, not wanting to bother the catering people.

When he entered the kitchen, he saw no one except a woman mixing drinks. His footsteps must have alerted her to his presence. She turned, took one look at him, and dropped her wine glass onto the floor, as well. She was wearing a one-piece leather dress with a plunging neckline that came with a kinky collar, buckle details, medical pockets and patches with wristlets. The skirt was extremely short, showing off her curvy legs in sexy fishnet stockings. She wore a black hat and a matching mask that covered her face down to her cheeks. Her eyes glittered, and her cherry lips were thick and lush. Darcy felt an instant attraction to her.

"Count Dracula!" the woman said breathlessly as she stared at him.

The Count heard her voice and recognised it immediately, but he played along. "And you are?"

"Mina," she whispered and dropped her gaze.*

He stared at her, willing her to look up at him again, but she didn't. Instead, hastily, she knelt to pick up the broken glass, and cut herself in the process.

"Ouch!"

He stepped forward, bent down and took her hand to inspect the injury. Two of her fingers were cut, but the wounds were minor. Still, there was blood. Reaching out, he raised her chin, willing her to protest or look at him. But she seemed determined to look away. So he put her fingers into his mouth and sucked them.

Mina gasped, finally returning his gaze.

Facing her boldly, he started licking her fingers. She breathed loudly in response, and her delectable breasts, cupped tightly together by the black dress, rose up and down in a quick rhythm.

All the while, he continued to enjoy her fingers as the atmosphere became more tense and electric. Then, decision made, he pulled her to stand, set aside the broken glasses, and took her out through the back door to where his car was parked, a few meters down the road.

She followed without a word.

He drove for several minutes until they reached a deserted country road. Stopping the car, he switched on the dome light and turned to gaze at her.

She turned, as well, and looked back at him with solemn intensity.

"You have allowed the Count to suck your blood. You are mine now?" he asked, voicing it as a question rather than a fact.

She nodded and whispered, "I would love to be yours."

Her words filled him with joy and relief. Smiling, he showed off his piercing teeth, then lowered his head and kissed her, using the elongated incisors to nibble lightly at her lips, her earlobe, her neck and her cleavage.

When he tried to open her dress, she said, "Shouldn't we continue in a more comfortable place?"

But the Count replied impatiently, "Wait? No. I have longed to devour you for months."

He pushed her back against the creamy leather seat and pressed a side button. The seat reclined. Then he tore open her dress and removed her mask. The plunging V shape in front broke at his force, and the skirt and the panties surrendered soon after. She did the same, unmasking him, then tearing open his shirt and pushing his trousers down impatiently.

Finally he had her naked except for the fishnet stockings, and she had him nude except for the cape. He lowered his teeth to graze upon her breasts, teasing the nipples into peaks while his hands traced over her smooth skin down to her secret valley. He parted the curls there and rubbed his thumb over her folds, making her squirm and moan.

She returned the favour, trailing her small hands over his torso, down to his stomach and manhood. She used both hands to encircle the thick shaft, stroking it from base to tip, squeezing and rubbing. He let out a loud cry under her ministration and parted her legs, then positioned himself at her entrance as he stared down at her. Slowly, she moved her hands from his shaft up to his hips and then his back. Smoothing her way over his skin, she cupped the clenched muscles of his backside, urging him on.

He needed no further confirmation, and pounded into her with a potent thrust. She screamed out loud, his huge arousal stretching her muscles to the limit.

After he had sunk to the hilt, he began the ancient ritual of mating, pushing into her like a man possessed by demons, shaking her to the core. In the closed car, their moans were loud, and the rough mating continued for an endless time until they both cried out, reaching their peaks. Her hands dug into his back, her nails scratching at him in a frenzy of delight, and she bit his shoulder as she climaxed. Convulsing, she squeezed him tightly, and he shivered, wrapping his hands around her pert bottom, holding her still, his captive, as he spilled his seed into her, on and on until the tremors ended.

They had no idea how long they had spent parked on the quiet country lane. When he returned to his senses, he asked softly, "Elizabeth, did you believe what I said in the email?"

"Yes. I'm sorry to have accused you so wrongly, and to have mistaken such unfounded statements as facts. And Charles has confessed that he was the one to blame. Now that he has made it up so sweetly to Jane, how can I blame you?"

"But what about your opinion of me?"

"Well, if my opinion had still been the same as before, I wouldn't have come to the party dressed as a night nurse," She smiled archly and added, "I came with blood for Count Dracula, too. It's in a bag in the medical pocket of my costume – wherever *that's* gotten to."

Darcy eyes lit up, truly delighted he had finally won the approval of this woman, and that she was ready to tease him.

"So, Bingley told you what costume I'd be wearing? And you lied. You are not Mina." Shifting, he reached down and searched her discarded costume. Finding the pocket, he took out the bag and looked at it closely. "That's not blood!"

"Poor Count! No blood to sustain you! But I think you will like this better." Her smile turned to a grin, and she winked at him.

He eyed the bag sceptically, glanced at her again, then tore open the bag. "Red condoms!" He smiled, flashed his piercing teeth.

Elizabeth nodded. "Yes. We forgot to use one just now, but what the hell! I am ready to resuscitate you when dawn comes, Count Dracula." She pushed him down onto the leather seat and gave him a rousing demonstration of mouth-to-mouth resuscitation.

***

*Flash back to three days before Halloween:*

"Anne, what are you doing?" George Darcy said to his wife.

"I'm looking at the crystal ball."

"You are checking up on Fitzwilliam again. You know that's not allowed except at the full moon."

"But he's grown up into such a lonely, serious man – nothing like the cheerful, happy young boy he used to be."

"I know. We both died too soon. Georgiana and the company are such a burden on him."

"And all the women! They are only after his money. None of them are interested in his heart. Luckily, Fitzwilliam is smart and has refused to be tempted by them. It's a good thing that he has Richard and Charles as his friends. I don't want him to be lonely. He is not young anymore, and he should be starting a family."

"Wow, that 'matchmaking mama' mentality doesn't die for women, even when they are living in heaven. Let him be. He has to choose his own destiny."

"But he loves this Elizabeth. We should cross over to help him."

"Cross over? You mean in a dream?"

"No, I hate dreams. I remember reading a story where an author wrote about the hero and heroine's long journey to happiness. It took the author many chapters, and the characters reached the age of 60 before they found each other again. Then, just before they were to be married, the hero died. I cried buckets and then, when I turned to the next page, you know what? All those previous chapters were just a dream! At that very instant, I developed a fervent dislike of dreams."

"Then how do you want to cross over?"

"I loved Mission Impossible – not Tom Cruise though. I mean the old TV series. Let's do a recording like this: 'These are instructions from your late mother and father. Carry them out or risk punishment from the other world. This recording will be destroyed in ten seconds'."

"You want to scare the hell out of our boy? What if you cause him a heart attack?"

"Posh! He is not some sissy to be frightened by hearing the voices of his parents. I will make it fun. Maybe I'll send him a code to decipher. He and Richard used to mess about with secret codes."

"You want to send him straight to this Elizabeth?"

"That would be too easy. Let's just send him out to socialise a bit. Lately, his life revolves solely around Pemberley and Georgiana."

"Then send him to Richard. He knows how to party."

"Richard is fine, but he likes to gossip. I think I will send him to Bingley. He is a cheerful chap and won't tease our boy too much."

"So your grand plan is to get Fitzwilliam out of Pemberley, and to let Bingley and him party together? How do you think he will end up with this Elizabeth?"

"As you said, he needs to choose his own destiny. What happens after that is up to him."

***

Darcy carried out his parents' instructions very well. He married Elizabeth half a year after the Halloween party, and they had three children together. As for the code, he forgot it in the car and never, in fact, deciphered it. But can you?

** Wilhelmina "Mina" Harker is a character in Bram Stoker's novel, Dracula. She was pursued by the Count in the novel.*

*And the message is "Go to the Halloween party, you will find your destiny there"*

*What if Caroline tried to ensnare Darcy by drugging him?*

## The Sexobot

Caroline B40 smiled smugly. Today would be her day, and it would end with her getting Sexobot Darcy into her bed.

Well, not exactly her own bed at Netherfield Base, but in the sumptuous bed here in Hunsford Deck.

She had forked out a fortune for the whole thing: the pills, the dinner and the suite. In the Austen galaxy, Collins W007 was the leading inventor of the male-ensnaring pill.

Collins's hypothesis was simple. It was a scientific fact that Martians were attracted to the opposite sex by their sense of smell. Therefore, if you wanted a male Martian to desire you, you needed to find out what scent excited him, then match it.

And she had. With the help of her hapless brother, Charles B44, she had managed to plant a miniscule temperature-tracking device on Darcy's neck. When Collins studied the data she had collected last November, he observed that Darcy's body temperature had shot up an average of 1.28 degrees every time he was near that trashy Eliza X88 from Meryton Planet.

Since the departure of the entire Martian party from that backwater planet, his body temperature had consistently registered below normal, a chill.

The next step had been as obvious as it was distasteful. She had paid a galaxy robber to steal some panties from Eliza, and asked Collins to examine the scent.

After five long months of waiting, Collins finally produced a unique set of pills which he called DPP – Darcy Possession Pills.

When Caroline took the pink one, it would to make her smell like Eliza. When she slipped the blue one into Darcy's drink, it would disturb his normal chemical balance. It would make him behave less like a Martian – calm and reserved – and more like an Earthling, passionate and expressive. And as Darcy was a Sexobot, once his chemical balance was disturbed, he would be like an addict, requiring several matings each day just to maintain his composure.

Laughing out loud, Caroline imagined having that power over him. She would withhold sex, in exchange for all the expensive gifts in the world, for Darcy was one of the richest men in the galaxy.

The execution of Caroline's plan began smoothly. When she and Darcy sat down for dinner, she sent her brother away on an errand, and slipped the blue capsule into Darcy's drink. Soon thereafter, however, the horrible Eliza X88 walked in, accompanied by her friend, Charlotte L54. Caroline swallowed the pink pill immediately, hoping that W007's invention would be enough to compete with the real scent of Eliza.

"Hello, Caroline. Nice to see you again, after so many months," Charlotte L54 said pleasantly. "Collins W007 invited me here to go over the results of his latest research project, and I brought my friend Elizabeth with me."

Suddenly, Darcy emitted an ear-piercing howl and jumped up from his chair. Pulling Caroline against his body, he sniffed her neck, then recoiled. "Yuck!" He sneezed and pushed her away roughly, sending her to the floor.

"What do you think you're doing?" Elizabeth demanded, and her voice drew his attention as she tried to help Caroline up.

Her attempt at a good deed was prevented when Darcy wrapped his arm around her waist. "I don't know." Pulling her tight to his chest, he drew in a deep breath. "Your scent! It's heavenly. I don't know what happened...but I don't think I can suppress my sexobotic functionality any more." With that, he threw her over his shoulders and rushed out of Hunsford Deck, heading toward the luxuriant spaceship of Rosings.

The angry voice of Caroline B40 and the concerned words of Charlotte L54 travelled to his ears as he made his mad dash. Nearer at hand, the arguments of Elizabeth X88 filled his head, as well, but he was beyond the point where mere words could waylay him.

"What is the meaning of this, nephew?" Catherine LD demanded, standing near the entrance.

"Get out of my way!" Sexobot Darcy said wildly. "Stand aside or be prepared to see me mate with X88 right in front of you. My sexobotic is triggered."

Catherine LD's face turned green. "Savage man!"

He pushed her out of the way, dashed into his suite and locked the door. Then he threw Elizabeth onto the huge waterbed.

"'Mate' with me? What do you mean your sexobotic is activated?" Elizabeth asked angrily.

But Darcy was beyond explanation and words. Tearing off his Martian robe, he exposed his broad shoulders, taut muscles and proud manhood. "I need to mate with you now or I will explode," he exclaimed, and threw himself on top of her.

She tried to twist away from him. "Let go of me, you arrogant Martian!"

"I can't." He grasped her face and rained hot, wet kisses over her eyes, cheeks and lips. "I think I may have been poisoned. I can't stop. Once my sexobotic functionality is triggered, I need to mate with the woman until I'm satisfied."

"Is that your pathetic excuse for forcing yourself on me?" She tried again to struggle free from him, but he was strong and desperate. Tearing off her spacesuit, he nibbled at her neck, shoulders and breasts.

"Tie me up!" he entreated, then lowered his mouth to suckle her nipples for a frantic minute before pulling away again. "Restrain me, or I won't be able to stop." With a tortured expression, he rolled away from her body and took a death grip on the headboard of the bed. "Quickly, tie me up!"

Realizing that he was serious, Elizabeth rolled away and dashed to grab his robe. Tearing it into hasty strips, she bound his right wrist to the bed post. But when she leaned across him in an effort to grasp his left hand, he eluded her and cupped her breast instead. His hot, caressing fingers seemed to burn against her skin. She moaned aloud.

Darcy's self-control shattered. With a single jerk, his right wrist broke free from the restraint. With both hands, he cupped and rubbed her exposed breasts, and her moaning became louder. When he pulled her higher so that he could suck at her nipples, she forgot all about the need to stop him.

Soon, he rolled her over on her back again and stripped the spacesuit off her body swiftly. "Please, Elizabeth, knock me unconscious now or I will force myself on you," he pleaded as he trailed his mouth and fingers down to her navel and apex.

Her fingers threaded through his hair, torn between yanking him away and pulling him closer. Her moment of hesitation allowed him to trace his tongue along her folds, causing her to shudder with need as blood rioted through her body.

As he licked and stroked her entrance, he murmured, "I've...loved you since I met you...in Meryton. But I don't want to...give way to my...instinct. It must be that...crazy Caroline B40 who...triggered my sexobotic. She...smelt of you, but with a small, underlying percentage of...rotting orange scent. Do you know...what it means...to be with a Sexobot Martian?"

"No...Yes...Don't talk...Darcy, just make me come!" Elizabeth gritted her teeth as she felt a climax building, stunned by the realisation that he was not yet even inside of her. How talented his tongue was!

When he threw her legs over his shoulders and started sucking her nub, she convulsed and reached her peak immediately. Wave after wave of hot fluid rushed to pool at the juncture of her thighs.

Darcy lowered her legs and positioned them around his waist. Brushing her bush and folds with ardent skill, he positioned himself at her entrance. She felt her soul coming down to earth, and she shivered at his ministration and trembled with anticipation.

With a flex of her legs, she invited him forward. At that, he groaned loudly and thrust his thick arousal all the way into her. She arched her body up to receive his forceful invasion. He was hot, hard and thick. When he slammed into her to the hilt, she felt as if she were reaching heaven again. Every inch of her inner core clasped possessively at his velvety shaft.

Then he lowered his upper body, kissed her hard on the mouth as his torso pressed against her breasts. Soon he raised his lower body, like a strong fish, and thrust forward and backward at speed, bombarding her muscles and womb with his presence. She had never felt such pleasure before. Every inch of her body, from head to chest to toe, was glued to him, except for the brief moments when he pulled back to enable himself to impale her even more deeply.

As the pleasure became too great to resist, she dug her finger nails onto his back and screamed with satisfaction. He stopped his thrusting then, allowing her to squeeze him tightly and savour the aftermath of the second orgasm, while he panted above her.

But he did not allow her to rest for long. Only a few minutes passed before he started pounding into her again. This time, he raised his upper body, braced himself on his elbows, and used his hands to worship her breasts. As her nipples were puckered hard, another wave of sensation cruised through her body. She squirmed and rubbed against him as he slammed into her, again and again, on and on. It took her two more orgasms before he came. When he burst, shooting his seed into her, he shivered and convulsed for ages, while her muscles were scorched with intense heat.

Over the next 24 hours, Sexobot Darcy awoke and mated with Elizabeth X88 countless times. Luckily, their body seemed to be made for each other, and she achieved climax after climax, no matter how many times he pounded into her or in what position.

Several attempts were made by Catherine LD, Caroline B40 and others to break open the door, but the structure of Rosings was built to last, and no one succeeded in disturbing the mating. Instead, the throes of passion inside the suite were clearly audible to everyone outside.

After a day, Darcy's urges finally dissipated, at least momentarily.

"What now?" Elizabeth asked. She was lying on top of him, and they were both exhausted.

"Do you not know about Sexobot Martians?"

She shook her head.

He grabbed a remote and switched on the computer so that she could read about his genetic composition.

As she reached the end of the article, her jaw dropped. "What are you telling me? That I've become your...your fix?"

"I'm afraid so, my dear, addictive Lizzy. If you don't let me mate with you, I will die of toxic frustration very soon."

"But how embarrassing! Your urges can come at any time of the day or night!"

"That's why we wear robes, to cover our bodies when I need to mate with you in public. But once we have a few children, my urges may be more controllable. I may be able to wait until we go back home before I demand sex with you," he speculated, with a grin and a blush.

"I'm going to kill B40!" she swore. "I don't even like you."

But she was a caring person. Taking pity on his well-being, she allowed him to stay and live with her. Gradually, she came to understand his character better. And he learned to cope with her loud, crude family.

His crazy sexobotic urges both endeared him to her and embarrassed her. They got married a few months afterwards, but their public display of affection did not stop until they had six children and were well into their old age.

As for Caroline B40, after the bitter disappointment of not ensnaring Darcy with DPP, she had a heart attack the first time she saw him mate with Elizabeth publicly at her dinner party. After that, she never could bear the sight of Martian men, and she lived a reclusive life.

# PRESENT

*What if the late Mr. Darcy left millions to Elizabeth?*

## The Imprudence of Anger

"Anne...?" George Darcy gasped for breath, making a visible effort to speak.

"Mom's okay. Don't talk, Dad. Try to rest." William Darcy looked bleakly down at his father, wondering how any man could hope to survive with so many tubes attached to his body.

"We quarrelled..." George Darcy continued. "...affairs...I... so sorry...leave... her...10....million pounds."

"What? To whom?" William asked, not understanding the intent of his father's words.

"Leave...money...to...Elizabeth...Ben......nach." With that, George Darcy drew his last breath and died.

William stared, in shock. How could his father die so suddenly? Just that afternoon, the whole family had gathered over lunch. And now he was dead. Darcy wouldn't be able to talk to him ever again.

And what had he been saying about an argument? Had Darcy heard correctly that his parents had had an argument about his father's...affairs? And that he wanted to leave money to one of his mistresses? But his father had always seemed utterly besotted with his wife!

Darcy clenched his fists, wondering how to break the news to his mother...if she ever woke. His parents had been driving from Pemberley to Matlock on the winding country lane when their car skidded off the road and plunged ten metres down the slope. Lady Anne had been unconscious ever since the crash.

Darcy was suddenly filled by a towering anger at the realisation that his father, George Darcy, had been a liar. How could he have told his son repeatedly of how he loved his wife every day of his life – and then confessed, on his deathbed, that he had a mistress? Darcy had always respected and looked up to his father. But it now appeared that his respect had been founded on a lie. His father had a mistress on the side. Worse yet, his last thoughts had been of her, wanting to provide for her.

In a fury, William resolved to ignore his father's instruction. No one else had been in the room when George Darcy breathed his last words. Let the mistress rot!

***

Nearly two months had passed since his father's death, but Darcy's mother was still unconscious. The doctor held out little hope that she would ever regain her senses. In the ensuing weeks, Darcy had been busy taking over the management of the company. His sister Georgiana had finally settled back at school, although extremely saddened by the accident and their family's loss.

That grief, coupled with the stress of the power struggle and responsibility for Pemberley Holding, had turned Darcy bitter and reserved. Sometimes, when he retired in the wee hours after a hard day of work, he would shut his eyes and think about how very kind George Darcy had been, and how Darcy had loved his father's mentoring. But those tender thoughts always ended with the bitter memory of that name, Elizabeth Benach. Then he would rage against his father, for dying early and cheating on his family.

He still planned to ignore this father's last wish but, today, he was furious with Caroline Bingley – again – and it led to something he couldn't ignore.

His father had hired Caroline half a year ago, largely because she was the daughter of his best friend, but it had become clear that she was just a shallow, scheming fortune hunter. Darcy frequently heard reports about the sloppiness of her work and her arrogant manner. Today, she had even tried to throw herself at him in the conference room, after a meeting, when everyone had left.

The way she had sat on the table and spread her legs in front of him made him sick. She hadn't even worn panties for the occasion. He'd nearly thrown up when he caught a glimpse of her no doubt well-used pussy. Begging him to stay, she had even had the audacity to say that she could help him mourn the loss of his father, since she had been one of the late Mr. Darcy's favourite girls.

Her words brought a haze to Darcy's eyes. *Don't tell me you were Father's mistress, too,* he thought angrily. Pushing her away, he had stalked back to his office like a man possessed, dialled security, and ordered them to escort her out of Pemberley Holding that instant.

Then, sickened by the interlude and his doubts, he tore the phone off the hook and threw it across the room. It struck the far wall, dislodging a large photograph of his parents looking tenderly at each other during the ground-breaking ceremony for PH, twenty years ago. The framed picture fell to the ground, the glass shattered, and the frame broke apart.

He rushed over and stomped on it several more times, to vent his fury. When he finally stopped to gasp for air, he noticed a smaller photo face-down in the midst of the photo frame's wreckage. Bending closer, he saw that the name *Elizabeth* was written on it, in George Darcy's bold handwriting.

He picked it up, his nostrils flared. Did he really want to know how his father's mistress looked like? He shook his head, tempted to tear the photo into a thousand pieces. But when had he ever turned his back on the truth?

Drawing a deep breath, he turned the photo around.

She was absolutely gorgeous. Not the blond, thin, celebrity type that was so common nowadays. This 'Elizabeth' was the exact opposite of Caroline Bingley. She looked healthy and voluptuous, petite and alive. In the photo, her long, curly brown hair was brushed by the wind. She was wearing a modest bikini in a green seascape, laughing as she played with a dog on a beach. Her skin looked tan and glowing.

Darcy felt as if he had been punched in the stomach. He wanted a woman like this, too -- someone to bring sunshine and laughter into his dull and stressful life. The young woman in this photograph was the very epitome of life.

He wanted to find her. He told himself that he would do it to honour his father's dying wish to make her rich. In his mind, however, he knew that he actually wanted to possess her. He needed to taste life again. Was that why his father betrayed his mother? Could he bear to lower his standards to bed such a woman? He didn't know the answer yet but he would soon. So decided, he went straight home and called George Knightley immediately.

It only took PH's security chief two days to find her.

"So quickly?" Darcy asked, not trying to hide his scepticism.

Knightley shrugged, unperturbed. "I have a friend at Scotland Yard. He helped me check the database for people named Elizabeth Benach."

Darcy frowned. "She has a record? Is that why you were able to find her so fast?"

"If she had record, it would just take him less than an hour," the security chief said. "No, he had to run through driver's licences instead. She's clean...and her last name is *not* Benach. That's why it took my friend two days."

Darcy's frown became deeper. "Not Benach? But that's what..." He stopped, not wanting to reveal the connection to his father.

"As I said, my friend ran the record first, with no luck. Then he tried the licence database, checking for Elizabeth Benach. But that didn't work either. So he started trying different variations on her surname – Bernard, Benak, and the like – until he found her. She's actually Elizabeth Bennet, 25 years old, and she works in hospitality."

So young! Darcy's eyes flared with anger as he asked scornfully, "An escort?"

Knightley wasn't sure why his boss was so determined to think ill of this woman. "As far as the Yard's records show, no. She manages her family's hotel, the Longbourn, in Ramsgate. But if you want me to make sure, I can go there and do a bit of snooping around." Knightley was intrigued, and wanted to learn the nature of her relationship with his strait-laced boss.

"No, that's all right. Just leave it, for the time being. Thanks," Darcy said quickly. If there was going to be a scandal, he preferred to discover it himself. He would go to Ramsgate himself, alone...

Well, no. On second thought, he wasn't easy among strangers. He would call his friend Charles, instead. Although he had fired Charles's sister Caroline, Darcy knew that Charles and his sister didn't get on well, and that Charles would still be his best friend.

"Fancy a holiday by the sea?" he asked when he reached Charles on the phone.

"Trying to get away from my shameless sister?" Bingley asked joyfully. "I'm all for ogling some sexy blond bikini girls in France."

Darcy rolled his eyes. "No, I'm thinking of home-grown beauties, this time. Have you ever been to Ramsgate?"

***

A week later, Darcy and Bingley stood on the doorstep of the Longbourn Hotel. Usually, Darcy stayed at luxurious hotels. In this case, he had been forced to tell a lie and claim that his personal assistant had messed up the booking. "Sometimes, it's good for us to stay in pigpens, if only to learn how the other half lives," he joked to Bingley.

"Well, then," a woman's voice teased, startling Darcy, "welcome to Longbourn, Mr. Piggy."

He turned, and found himself facing the woman who had haunted his dreams for the past few weeks. Clearly, the photo hadn't captured half of her vitality. Her eyes sparkled with anger and cynical laughter. Her lush lips were pursed in an unconscious pout. She was wearing a bikini, this time yellow in colour, and her hair and skin were still wet. She had a darker tan, fuller breasts, a narrower waist and wider hips than in the photo. Darcy felt heat rush to his face and twist in his stomach. He wanted to throw her over his shoulder, take her to his cave and possess her for the rest of the day.

"Lizzy, stop it!" a gentle voice chided, breaking in on Darcy's thoughts. "I'm sorry, sir. My sister likes to tease.

Do you have a booking?" asked a tall woman with long blond hair.

Bingley's eyes lit up. "Yes, we do. William Darcy and Charles Bingley," he said with a grin, his gaze fixed solely on the gentle angel.

"Oh, yes! I remember. For two weeks, in two of our best rooms. Thank you, sir, for staying in our family hotel. I'm Jane Bennet, and this is my sister, Elizabeth," she said softly to Bingley. "I'll prepare for your check-in." She moved to the counter, and Bingley followed after her.

Left behind, Darcy returned his stare to Elizabeth.

She arched her eyebrows and walked toward the back of the hotel, with a teasing departing song. "Little piggy bit his tongue...little piggy sealed his lips..."

Darcy suppressed a smile as his gaze followed her skipping steps. She didn't sway her hips like most models would when they walked in front of him. But her striding form made her pert bottom bounce in a tantalising rhythm.

He needed a cold shower, now!

No, he needed the truth, quickly!

***

Darcy was increasingly glad that he had had the foresight to bring Bingley along, especially when Charles announced that the next day was Jane and Elizabeth's day off, and that he had arranged for Darcy and himself to join them on the beach.

At the water's edge, while Bingley was getting to know Jane, Darcy stretched out on a towel at a safe distance that was, nonetheless, still within earshot. Elizabeth, by comparison, made it clear that she had no time for the ‘arrogant man’, and busied herself making sand castles near the shoreline.

His hope of learning more about Elizabeth from her sister was soon rewarded, and he listened to Bingley and Jane's conversation with keen interest.

"So, you have five sisters?" Charles asked.

"Yes. Father died when I was twenty-two, and Lizzy took over the running of the hotel, since she had studied accounting and management," Jane explained calmly.

"I'm sorry to hear about your loss."

"No, no, it's fine. That was five years ago, and Father was never one to encourage sadness. Lizzy has been great. She and Father were very close, but she perked up and took control immediately when the bank announced that it wanted to call in the loan earlier."

"That must have been a tough time for the whole family."

"Mama was crying most of the time, and Mary, Kitty and Lydia were still in school. I felt lost and overwhelmed, but Lizzy marched into town and talked to the bank. Then she changed her course work from full-time to part-time, and also got some marketing and the website for the hotel going. She managed to turn the business around within months."

"I'm sure you helped your sister a lot, as well."

Jane smiled. "We're very close. She likes to run her ideas by me, first. She always jokes that she represents the bad customers and I represent the nice ones. But really, she doesn’t have a mean bone in her body. She even took a cooking course, so that she can fill in if the chef takes leave suddenly."

Darcy listened to this litany of information with disbelief, as he watched Elizabeth from afar. She appeared to have covered her tracks well, not even letting her sister know about her sordid affair. Had she become

George Darcy's mistress for the benefit of her bereaved family? If so, could he forget about that and make her his?

When he saw that the object of his suspicion had abandoned her castle and gone into the water for a dip, he decided to confront her. With decided strides, he walked down the beach and into the water until it reached his thighs, then dove beneath the surface of the water.

It was cold and refreshing. Within a few strokes, he surfaced at her side, close enough to breathe in her invigorating lavender scent. He stared at the mane of curly hair which framed her lovely face, then looked lower, to the line where the water lapped at the creamy flesh of her upper arms and breasts. That bewitching sight made him forget about his anger. Darcy uttered his thoughts spontaneously, without thinking. "You look lovely."

Elizabeth looked at him uncertainly, and her face turned crimson. "Thank you," she murmured.

He raised his hand and brushed the wet, unruly curls away from her forehead. With the backs of his fingers, he caressed her cheek and traced his way down to her jaw as he eyed her tempting lips. "May I?" he asked softly.

Her sparkling eyes returned his intense gaze for a long minute. Then she leaned toward him, ever so slightly, and her luscious lips parted.

Darcy was mesmerised. His body drifted toward her, and his mouth sought her welcoming one. Her lips were plump, and tasted of chocolate and mint.

He was instantly addicted. Deepening the kiss, he enjoyed her passionate response. By the time he let go of her delectable mouth to draw an essential breath, his hands had drifted down from her waist to cup her pert bottom. To his astonished gratification, he felt her hands toy with the waistband of his swimming trunks, then grasp his buttocks.

"Mr. Darcy!" she said breathlessly.

Those two words – which were his name but had also been his father's – struck him like a fierce lightning bolt slashing through a night-black sky, startling him back to his senses. His physical desire for her fled, leaving him feeling sickened by her, and by himself for wanting her.

He had to crack open her disguise, to expose her shortcomings. Then he could take her as his, on his own terms, openly. "Where did you get the money to turn away the bank?"

She blinked twice in surprise at his sudden shift in tone. "What do you mean?"

"Did my father give you the money?"

"Your father?" she queried, her expression one of puzzlement.

"Yes. George Darcy of Pemberley Holding. Don't pretend you don't know him. His dying words were about you," He spat out the words with a vengeance, remembering the pain of the day his father died. "How did you suck the old man in?"

Elizabeth's breathing grew agitated, pushing her lovely chest up and down against the lapping water. "You bastard! What are you accusing me of? Did you kiss me just to spite me? I don't even know your father."

She tried to pull away from him. But he wrapped his arms around her more tightly, causing her struggling form to rub against his body, stirring his arousal. "He paid you money to hold off the bank, didn't he?" He barked the words out, inches from her face. "He left you ten million pounds, his dying wish, for services rendered. So tell me," he sneered, "just how long did you 'serve' him?"

Her eyes narrowed. "I don't know your father. Let go of me or I'll scream."

"Scream for what? Bingley and your sister have gone off. The beach looks deserted."

She glanced back at the beach.

"You want to scream? I'll make you scream – from ecstasy," he swore and captured her mouth with his own.

After a few moments of struggle, she began to return his kiss with ardour, and her fingers flexed, squeezing his butt cheeks.

The fingers of his right hand slipped inside her bikini top and captured the hardened nipple hidden there. He thrust his tongue into her mouth and used the pad of his thumb to torment her cherry tip.

Her hands were busy, as well, pushing his swimming trousers down. He struggled out of them, shivering in anticipation, waiting for her to caress his length. Instead, he suddenly felt a searing pain in his groin. Wrenching away from her, he cried out in pain.

"Rot in hell!" she growled, and quickly swam away from him, taking his swim trunks with her.

Darcy could do nothing. He had to let the pain to subside. Finally reality sank in. He gritted his teeth. That bloody Elizabeth Bennet had left him on a deserted beach, naked!

***

“What have you been up to?” Knightley asked.

“What do you mean?”

“I mean that Elizabeth Bennet is demanding to see you, immediately.”

Darcy folded his arms, torn between anger and excitement. Six frustrating months had passed since his trip to Ramsgate, when he had last seen her. Since then, he had gone out with more women than he could count but none of them had progressed past a dinner date. They had all been con artists, too fawning, too obvious, and entirely too eager to have sex with him, if he was willing. The result was that they had all totally turned him off. None of them could begin to compare to Elizabeth.

Of course, he was still fuming over his encounter with her, half a year ago. It had been, without question, the most humiliating experience of his entire life, that day on Ramsgate Beach.

After Elizabeth swam away with his swimming trunks, he had waited in the water for nearly half an hour before Bingley reappeared. During that time, a few man-hungry women had come near and tried to chat him up. He had given them a cold scowl, but it didn't deter them. In the end, he'd had to swim for his life and dignity, to keep them from seeing that he was naked below the water line.

By the time Bingley returned with Jane Bennet, Darcy was exhausted. He had to call Bingley out into the water, alone, and explain his need for a new pair of trunks. His normally easy-going friend asked far too many questions before he went back, accompanied by Jane, to fetch the essential garment for him. Although Darcy had chosen not to reveal Elizabeth's relationship with his father, he had been forced to admit to Bingley that he had insulted her, before his friend would agree to do his bidding.

Gallingly, Darcy was sure that Bingley had told Jane about the incident. It took his friend an awfully long time to return from the hotel. Darcy was forced to avoid three more inquisitive women in the water while he waited.

When the duo finally returned to the hotel, Jane was angry with Darcy, as well – apparently because Elizabeth had told her something. As soon as he appeared, the eldest Bennet asked him to leave the hotel. Bingley was torn, not sure if he should leave or stay. Darcy insisted that he stay, as he wanted an excuse to come back to Elizabeth. For the moment, however, he'd known that he would have to ring his personal assistant and ask her to find him another hotel in Ramsgate urgently.

That next day, six months ago, he welcomed Elizabeth into a private conference room at a five-star hotel. He had gone back to the Longbourn Hotel to ask for her, earlier that day. Although Jane was reluctant to pass on the message, he had used his billionaire persona to threaten her. When an angry Elizabeth came out to face him, he told her that he had a secret document back at his hotel, ready for her to sign if she wanted the money from his father's estate. He delivered the news coldly, and she looked at him for a long time, her expression of anger slowly mellowing. He silently willed her to turn his offer down...but she didn't. She agreed to come to his hotel in an hour's time.

Elizabeth came alone, in a stunning, flirty dress which accentuated her every curve. Sporting bright red lipstick and crimson fingernails, she swayed into the room on dangerously high heels.

Darcy swallowed hard and drew in a deep breath. He knew that he needed to keep his cool if he was going to negotiate the transaction to his satisfaction.

"The ten million pounds will be transferred from my personal account into yours in four equal instalments over the next twelve months. I own a public company worth billions, so I can't afford to have the media suspect anything. My affairs are reported on closely by the tabloids."

Elizabeth raised her eyebrows and smiled at him seductively. She took a long time to read the document, which demanded that she maintain total secrecy about how she had obtained the money, most particularly agreeing not to divulge that it had been provided by the late Mr. Darcy according to his death wish.

When Elizabeth took up the pen and signed the document, anger shook Darcy to his core. He had still harboured a fantasy that she would refuse the money and denounce her relationship with George Darcy, but her action killed his naïve hope.

"Fine," he forced himself to say. "The first instalment will be deposited into your bank account tomorrow. Now, here is the second document." He produced another paper from his briefcase and placed it on the table between them with a loud slap of his hand. "Sign it and you will have all the designer clothes and a jet-setting existence for the rest of your life. I assume that you will sift through the ten million dollar bequest very quickly. Think of this as your back-up plan."

She took her time reading through the clauses of the second document, then said, "So...you want me to become your mistress? And in return you are offering this huge sum of money, clothes, holidays, houses every year until such time as I can't please you any more. Your lawyers were exceptionally thorough, defining what would constitute my 'acceptable behaviour,' anticipating the event of a child, specifying what will happen to me if I cheat on you, or if either of us dies suddenly. Were they screenwriters before they became lawyers? Their imagination seems to be boundless."

"Count yourself lucky that I'm in lust with you."

"So much in lust that you are willing to take 'used merchandise' from your father?" She spoke the disgusting sentence with a smug smile.

He rose from the chair and walked to the window, forcing himself to stare out at nothing. He had to get away from her, or he would grab her and kiss her senseless. "Leave my father out of this. You have the ten millions from that episode of your life. Once you sign the second document, a new chapter begins. Your body will belong to me, at any time of the day and night. Your thoughts will concentrate on me, and on me alone."

She chuckled. "And such wonderful thoughts they would be!"

Darcy gripped the window sill. Surrendering to his lust would be one thing. But he wouldn't surrender his soul to her sparkling, twisted personality.

Behind him, he heard the rustle of paper and the sound of the pen scratching along as she signed. He clinched the window even tighter and gritted his teeth. *How can I possess her, every day, knowing that she can be bought? I hope I can get tired of her, after just one night...*

The noise of a slamming door made him turn around. She had left the room! He owned her now, so where the bloody hell was the infuriating woman? He went to the desk, intending to stuff the signed contract backs into his briefcase and chase after her. But large writing scrawled diagonally over the text of the document caught his eyes. Elizabeth had ignored the signature line and, instead, had written "FUCK YOUR MONEY" across his second contract.

He stared at it for ages. So? She didn't want to be his mistress. She was content to live with the ten millions from his father. Had she loved his father so much?

That question, and the image of Elizabeth with his father, had haunted him during every day of the past six months. But now, suddenly, she had demanded to see him. What did she want? Had she burned through the ten million pounds already? Was she coming back to beg him to take her as his mistress, after all? His dormant body roused at the prospect. He wanted her, naked, beneath him, begging for his mercy.

***

"How can I help you?" he asked, and his voice trembled.

She was even more beautiful than before, although she was wearing an old t-shirt and a pair of jeans, without any jewellery. She looked utterly out of place in his grand, sombre office. When she came to a halt in front of his massive desk, he could see that she looked thinner than before, and that shadows lurked beneath her eyes. But the changes didn't make her any less attractive to him. In fact, the subtle signs of vulnerability stirred his protective instincts. He wanted to hold her and promise her eternity.

No, he wouldn't think in those terms. After all, she had accepted his father's money.

Elizabeth bit her lower lip, then removed a photograph from the envelope she held, and slammed it onto his desk.

Not so vulnerable after all.

"What's this?" he asked, his eyes focused on her, not the photograph.

"Look at it!" she ordered, and her eyes flamed with fire.

He leaned forward and spared it a quick glance. Then his heart skipped. Grabbing it up, he looked at it more closely. It was a very old photo, and it showed a handsome man hugging a gorgeous woman on a street.

"But...I don't understand," he said. "That's Alan Bingley..." His voice trailed off into silence.

"...and my mother!" Elizabeth continued.

"Your mother?"

She nodded. Taking another document out of the envelop, she held it out to him.

It turned out to be an investigation report from a private detective company. Darcy scanned it quickly, not needing to read through it completely because understanding had already begun to dawn on him. He had long known that Bingley's late father had been a playboy. "Alan Bingley had an affair with your mother?"

She nodded sharply, produced yet another piece of paper out, and threw it onto the table. "Here is what remains from the payments from your father's bequest. I only took enough to hire a private detective. You can cancel the rest of the instalments. I don't know why your father left me the money. Perhaps he thought it would be an untraceable way to help Alan Bingley do so. Whatever the reason, I don't want any of it. Alan Bingley was never my father in any emotional sense. I have everything I'll ever need in Longbourn," she spoke firmly, and turned to leave.

Darcy came around the desk and chased after her. Stopping her by the door, he felt a thrill of relief race through his body. She was not his father's mistress! She never had been! "I'm sorry, Elizabeth."

"Are you?" she challenged, her eyes wide with anger.

"Yes." He couldn't explain more. How could he make her understand the pain brought on by the sudden death of his father, of seeing his mother on life support, or of the immense pressure of stepping into his father's shoes? Raising his hand, he caressed her cheek, trying to convey his unspoken emotions through the intensity of his gaze.

Elizabeth was panting. The flame in her eyes dimmed slightly, and tears welled up. "You thought I was a whore!" she said, and her voice cracked with pain.

"I was angry." He wrapped his arms around her waist and rested his chin on her head. "Angry with Dad for dying. He was only in his late fifties. We should have had so many more years together. How could he leave my mother, Georgiana and I alone in this world? How could his last thought have been of someone else? How could his focus have been on providing a faceless woman with money? Caroline – Caroline Bingley – is Charles's younger sister, and my father let her work here. She tried to seduce me. She was shameless, and it couldn't have been clearer that she was only after my money. I was so angry that I broke something in my office – and that's when I discovered your photo. You looked so full of life, so blissful. I became furious with you, too. It was as if your happiness fuelled my anger." His confused explanation tumbled out. He didn't know whether he was making any sense or not. He was just happy to be holding Elizabeth so tightly.

"You've crushed me," she murmured.

He thought that she meant it in a physical sense, and so he loosened his embrace reluctantly and took a step back. But that enabled him to gaze into her expressive eyes, and he instantly understood that she meant emotionally, not physically. "I'm so sorry," He assured her, his voice full of remorse.

She took an unsteady breath. "You're the most interesting man I've ever met. You fixed that intense gaze on me, the first two days we met. I thought you were interested in me, romantically. My heart was on Cloud Nine. But then, on the beach, all of your contempt came pouring out. It was enough to drown me. My heart felt as if you were grinding it into powder. That's when I realised that I was just a slut in your eyes. You thought I'd sold my body to your father. My five years of hard work to turn Longbourn around, and all of my proud achievements were nothing to you. It tore me to pieces." A single tear slid down her face.

He used his thumb to wipe it away, utterly ashamed of himself. This wonderful, diligent, beautiful woman had wanted to open her heart to him. And what had he done? His rage had turned him into a beast, and he had stomped on her heart, repeatedly. He had accused her of whoring her way to success, and then he had offered her the most degrading possible offer. In writing. A 'mistress' contract. How could he deny it when he still had it locked in his safe? "Can you ever forgive me?" Darcy cried in despair.

Dropping his hands, he moved away from her, walking like a defeated man. Slumping onto the sofa, he cradled his head in his hands and muttered, "Oh my God, Dad, I messed up the only good thing that came my way after you died. You must be disgusted with me!" With that, tears overcame him, for the first time since his father's death. More words of torment poured out. "I'm worthless! With all the money in the world, I couldn't save you. Mom is still in a coma. Georgiana is solemn and depressed. The company is doing all right, but why didn't I use the money to investigate the matter further, before accusing Elizabeth? I'm not worthy of being your son, Dad! I'm nothing but an ugly beast," Darcy berated himself, speaking aloud the words he so wished he could address to his father.

It was then that he felt her hand gently pushing the hair back from his forehead. Elizabeth knelt in front of him and kissed the tears from his face. "No. That's not so. You're a good man," she murmured. "You truly love your parents and your sister. After losing your father, and in spite of all that you have suffered, you've done a great job of handling the business affairs of Pemberley Holding. I've learned more about you, from Charles."

He gasped for air and turned, tear-blinded, to kiss her face. "I have to confess to you, I love you, Elizabeth. I fell in love with you almost immediately after I met you. Your lively spirit and your hard-working attitude are what I've always craved in a partner. But I messed up everything, throughout our acquaintance. Can you forgive me, Elizabeth?"

She nodded and continued to kiss away his tears.

"Will you give me another chance? A chance to start over?" he entreated, his voice full of vulnerability.

"Yes," she replied with conviction. "A new beginning."

***

Fast-forward thirty years. Beneath a sky bright with stars, at the far end of the beach in Ramsgate, an 'elderly' couple giggled like teenagers.

"William, we can't do this!" Elizabeth laughed merrily as she pushed her husband's roving hands away.

"Why not?" Darcy challenged, and licked her earlobe.

"Because we're the parents of the bridegroom. What if someone from the wedding party comes down for a midnight dip and finds us making out, in the water? You're over sixty years old now. You're supposed to behave as an elderly gentleman should."

"Elderly? I'm simply mature!" He scowled, then nudged her bikini bottom aside, sliding two fingers between her folds, aiming for her G-spot. "I'm as fit as I was when we first met. And you, my very dear, will have to pay for calling me elderly," he growled, and lowered his mouth to suckle her nipple, just the way she loved.

The past thirty years had been a joy to the Darcys, except for the occasional explosive rows that every spirited couple experienced. They had four wonderful children – three boys and a girl. Pemberley Holding had grown bigger and better. And, today, their eldest Andrew, who was now the head of PH, was getting married in Ramsgate.

Indeed, Ramsgate was the place where many of the important occasions in the Darcy family had taken place.

After their emotionally draining confrontation in Darcy's office, thirty years ago, Elizabeth and he had become an item. He'd learned a bit more about her parentage, and Mrs. Bennet had then filled in some further details after Elizabeth confronted her with the report from the private detective.

Mrs. Fanny Bennet suffered post-natal sickness for nearly a year after Jane was born, but Mr. Bennet was too busy with the hotel to notice her difficulty. Alan Bingley had come to Ramsgate for a development project, and his charm brought Fanny back to life. When Alan moved on, a month later, without so much as a goodbye, Fanny found herself pregnant and confessed the affair to Mr. Bennet. Her husband was remorseful of his neglect and forgave her indiscretion. In fact, he doted on Elizabeth when she was born, even more so than on Jane. Lizzy was the precious little gift who had brought Fanny back to her old self for him.

As for the involvement of Darcy's father, Elizabeth and her husband were unable to solve the mystery of it until Lady Anne miraculously awoke from her coma, a year after the traffic accident. She told them, then, that her beloved George had been entrusted with finding Alan Bingley's love child when the latter died. Fanny Bennet had informed Alan of Elizabeth birth, many years ago, but the playboy had never felt the need to get in touch with her, and had lost contact. Only when he was faced with his own mortality did Alan crave absolution. He transferred ten millions pounds, secretly, from his personal accounts to George Darcy for Elizabeth’s benefit, because Mrs. Bingley was a shark, and Alan was afraid that she would try to harm Elizabeth financially and emotionally. But Lady Anne didn't approve of her husband's involvement in keeping this secret from Bingley's children, and, sadly, they had argued about it yet again in the car, which led to the traffic accident.

Elizabeth and Darcy's marriage, soon after these revelations, brought joy to the recovering Lady Anne. Darcy continued to mellow, throughout the ensuing years, as he became accustomed to the tender teasing of his wife. Their marriage, sweet from the onset, deepened into a true partnership. They shared their worries, laughter, tears and hopes, every day. And their physical relationship was of the most passionate nature. Indeed, they couldn't keep their hands off each other. A certain look, a particular association, or a special memory was enough to convince Mr. and Mrs. Darcy to hide away from the public and pursue their bonding.

This late night swim was just the most recent example. After the wedding of their son, Elizabeth had laughed at Darcy, remembering how she had kept his swimming trunks for months after stranding him on the beach without them during their first anger encounter. Now, all these years later, she convinced him to run down the beach with her for a midnight dip.

"Just be careful, Mrs. Darcy," he murmured as he wrapped Elizabeth's legs around his waist.

"Of...what?" Her words were hardly recognisable, as she was moaning in ecstasy. His fingers explored her sex with fierce skill, driving her ever nearer to the edge.

"Don't...push off...my swimming trunks." Darcy breathed out the words with difficulty as he slowly pushed into her hot, welcoming core. "I don't want to have to wait here... naked, hoping for rescue again." Her muscles gripped his manhood, creating a stimulating friction that shot shivers through his body. Elizabeth's lustful cries flooded his ears, goading him into a frantic thrusting rhythm. He pounded into her delicious body, on and on, again and again, until she cried out in elation. He reached his own climax soon afterwards.

Slowly, their breathing returned to normal but Darcy, to his consternation, found that he had jostled off his swimming trunks during their blazing love-making. They spent some time searching for the vanished garment in the water, but in vain. Luckily, however, Mrs. Darcy had had the foresight to bring along a change of clothes, thus saving Mr. Darcy from the predations of any man-eating females who might have been lurking on the beach in search of a sugar daddy.

*What if Mr. Darcy received a special gift?*

## Santa in the Cake

"I can't fit into the costume!" Elizabeth said, and scowled in frustration.

She was supposed to be the elf, with Kitty as Santa Claus at the gig. But Kitty had done a runner in the past hour. She was going to a party with Lydia. Mary had to step in, but she had flatly refused to be the sexy Santa, so Elizabeth had taken on the role.

But the skimpy dress was far too short for her. And her cup size could hardly be contained inside an outfit made for her flat-chested sister.

"Oh, stop wiggling! I'm using safety pins to fix it." Mrs. Bennet smacked Elizabeth's hands away from the lapel and continued, "The birthday boy certainly won't mind if our new Santa has a bit more flesh showing."

"Just remember, this is the last time I will help," Elizabeth said, gritting her teeth to endure her mother's vulgar eagerness.

"Oh, hang your boring job. As if you'd ever meet rich men by working inside a lab with all those rods," Mrs.

Bennet retorted. "I run Longbourn Wishes for you girls, and – guess what? – the one time that Charlotte filled in for Lydia, she snared Billy Collins."

"They're test tubes, not rods." Elizabeth rolled her eyes. "And Charlotte is perfectly welcome to have a thousand Billies." Mr. Collins might be considered rich in the wallet according to her mother's standard, but to Elizabeth he was definitely poor in both manner and wit.

"Anyway, Jane's doing very nicely with Charles," Mrs. Bennet continued. "This is his friend's referral. It's the first time we got a gig in Rosings. Twenty-four bedrooms! Their guests must be super-rich, too. Just make sure you mingle with them, show a bit of cleavage, and you'll be set for life."

"Charles should shut Longbourn Wishes down, not refer jobs to you," Elizabeth retorted, then swore under her breath as her mother finished fastening the dress tightly together.

"Go, go, go," Mrs. Bennet said as she shooed Mary and Elizabeth out of the door, but she smiled smugly as she locked up behind them, because she hadn't told her second daughter that she used very old pins – and not many of them – to hold the lapels together. The chances were good that they would burst before the evening was out. And the belt buckle was old, too. *Well, it's all for her own good*, she thought.

Half an hour later, when Mary and Elizabeth arrived at Rosings, they were greeted by a tall, fine man. He was not handsome but friendly.

"Richard here. And you are?" He ogled at Elizabeth's long rain coat suspiciously and shook her hand warmly.

"Santa Claus from Longbourn Wishes," Elizabeth replied in her stern scientist's voice. She hated leering men. At least this one was not the birthday boy, since he was greeting them. She wouldn't have liked to sing for him.

"She's Lizzy and I'm Mary," said her sister.

"Good. You'll be working separately tonight. Miss Mary, you're for the staff quarters. And our dear old boy will just love a visit from Santa." He grinned like an idiot as he continued to look Elizabeth over from top to toe.

An elderly lady, around 60 years old, came out to greet them. "Richard, you take the elf to the staff quarters, and I'll show Santa to her waiting place." She held out her hand to Elizabeth. "Hello. I'm Mrs. Reynolds. You must be Lizzy."

"Yes." Elizabeth felt a tiny bit more relaxed upon seeing the kind-looking woman. She wouldn't want to be left alone with that Richard. "You're a friend of Charles's?"

"Yes, I've known Charles since he was a little boy." She walked Elizabeth to the library. Once they were inside, she took Elizabeth's coat and hung it up by the door.

"You want me to surprise the birthday boy in the library? It's not a birthday party?" Elizabeth took a quick glance around and was not impressed. The library was huge but untidy. There was a mahogany desk and chair in the corner on the right-hand side. To its right sat a big chesterfield sofa in burgundy. Books on the shelves were in disarray. She didn't feel comfortable being left alone in such a secluded room with a man, dressed as she was in such a sexy outfit. What if he was drunk?

"Our dear old boy has been feeling rather low, lately. This is the only room he frequents, aside from his bedroom. Anyway, he's the quiet type. He doesn't like to mix with strangers, so we don't want to make him uncomfortable with a party. He likes oldies songs, Frank Sinatra and the like, you know. So we came up with the idea to hire someone to sing for him, give him a private concert. There is the cake." Mrs. Reynolds chatted on as she led Elizabeth around the last shelf, where there was a giant cake, roughly waist-high, adorned with beautiful icing and decorations.

She turned one of the carrots and continued. “Let me unlock the cake for you so that you can hide inside. You’ll see that the inside is made of wood. You’ll need to squeeze in a bit, but there are two peep holes, so you can see him come in, at least from the waist down. Then you push open this top lid and give him a surprise. Here is an iPod with some of his favourite music. Do you want to try the locks?”

Elizabeth looked at the cake sceptically. It looked a bit too small for her to fit inside. But, when she gave it a try, it did work. When she crouched down, Mrs. Reynolds could close the door easily.

Through the peep holes, she could see the waist of the elderly lady. Then she unlocked the lock of the top lid and stood up. The cake was positioned in such a way that it had a very limited view of the desk. And the last two bulbs of the ceiling lights by this row of shelves had burned out. Or perhaps someone had deliberately unscrewed them, so that the cake could sit in semi-darkness. The birthday boy wouldn’t be likely to see it unless he walked very close by.

“Perfect!” Mrs. Reynolds said. “Now, try opening the door on the side of the cake, to make sure you can step out. But if it sticks, you can still ask him to pull you out from the top. Just make sure you don’t step on the cake icing. The outside layers are real cake, and we plan to distribute them to the staff and their families, tomorrow.”

Elizabeth nodded and unlocked the door. It worked, which was a relief since she doubted whether the elderly Mr. Reynolds could pull her out from the top of the cake if the lock was stuck.

“Wonderful! I’ll bring in a few of his favourite dishes and put them on the side table. And there’s champagne in the mini-bar. When he comes in, just sing him a few songs, and then come out to join us in the staff quarters, afterwards. You don't need to stay and eat with him," she said.

Elizabeth nodded again and she settled down inside the cake. Mrs. Reynolds and her family had certainly gone to a lot of trouble to cheer up her husband. The cake must have cost a fortune to make. But Elizabeth shook her head over the idea of hiring a young sexy Santa to sing for her husband. She admired Mrs. Reynolds's courage. It was lucky that Kitty had skipped this job, since she couldn't carry a tune.

Wryly, Elizabeth thought about her mother's hopes. She wouldn't be meeting any rich guests of marrying age tonight, probably just a grumpy old man! Anyway, she didn't need to find a man yet. At least, that was what she kept telling herself.

Before long, she heard footsteps and saw Mrs. Reynolds coming back. Was she bringing in the food? "I'll go now," the woman said. "He won't be long. He just rang to say he's on his way home from work."

"Okay," Elizabeth replied. Poor Mrs. Reynolds! Her husband worked on Christmas Eve and his birthday.

She sorted through the contents of the iPod and decided to select a cheerful song to start. She had been musing about old age and life in darkness for a quarter of an hour before she heard footsteps again. As she peeked out from the peep holes, she saw the legs of a man wearing a navy blue business suit walk in. He seemed surprisingly fit, with no need for a walking stick.

As soon as he turned away with his back to the cake, possibly looking at the food on the side table, Elizabeth pressed the button to start the music, then pushed open the lid and began to sing, in her cheeriest tones:

*You better watch out*

*You better not cry*

*Better not pout*

*I'm telling you why*

*Santa Claus is coming...*

She stopped dead in the middle of the sentence when she saw the man had had spun around and was now walking toward her.

"Elizabeth!"

"Dr. Darcy!"

They stared at each other, both turning crimson.

"Umh...what are you doing here?" Elizabeth asked. She hadn't seen him at all in the month or more since the incident.

"Umh...This is my aunt's house. We're staying here for the holidays." He squinted in the dim light, gazing at her attire. Then he swallowed hard. It reminded him of that incident. "What are *you* doing here?"

"Well... My mother has this event company. I'm filling in for one of my sisters. I was supposed to surprise Mr. Reynolds. It's his birthday." She diverted her gaze, mortified at being found wearing an almost indecent outfit.

"Mr. Reynolds?" He frowned. "But he's not here. And his birthday is in April. Tonight is *my* birthday, actually..."

"Oh...? Oh! Charles did this to me!" She finally got it. "I'm going to kick his ass when I catch up with him," she said, and took a deep, agitated breath.

In that instant, the safety pins and the belt broke open.

Two pairs of eyes dropped to look at Elizabeth's body. The yellow lacy bra, matching panties and stockings were fully on display. Darcy devoured the sight, wishing the lights were brighter. Meanwhile, Elizabeth's whole body turned bright red with embarrassment. It took her several seconds to absorb the shock, as she tried – with minimal success – to pull the Santa suit closed again.

Darcy shifted his weight from one leg to the other, then started to take off his jacket.

"What are you doing?!" she demanded breathlessly, on the edge of panic. His broad muscle pushed against the thin shirt. She remembered how she had dug her fingers into his chest as he had pumped into her again and again on that unforgettable night, a month ago. She could still remember the sensation of his magnificent shaft filling her up. It had been scorching hot, hard and earth-shattering.

"I'm...giving you my jacket. So you can cover up."

"Oh."

He considered her predicament. "Do you want to come...out of the cake?" he asked, not wanting to hand his jacket over to her quite yet. He was still savouring the sight of her curvaceous figure.

She nodded. With one hand clenched to secure the Santa outfit, she used the other to press the lock. But it didn't work. The door wouldn't open.

She fumbled a few more times with one hand. Then she got so frustrated that she abandoned her efforts to close her dress and used both hands to shake the lock.

Still it wouldn't move.

Darcy gazed at her, taking in her long, wavy hair and the shaking of her luscious form. He could still remember sucking her sweet nipples and squeezing her pert buttocks as he had plunged into her for what seemed like forever, that night. Her skin was smooth, soft and burning, and he had enjoyed the most amazing climax of his life. Over the past month, he had relived that memory over and over again, always with the same result. Even now, the thought was so potent that he had to drape his jacket over his hand to disguise his newly aroused body.

"It's stuck!" Elizabeth exclaimed, and bit her lip.

"You can't get out?"

"You can pull me out from the top. We just need to make sure we don't step on the icing." She took another deep breath, trying to calm herself, and saw that his eyes were focused on her breasts, where the dress hung open. Grimly, she tried to close the dress again.

Walking to the edge of the cake, Darcy dropped the jacket and reached over to put his hands on her waist. "Brace your hands on my shoulders," he instructed in a husky voice, feeling as if an electric current were running through his body.

She did as she was told, which caused the Santa dress to open once again.

No longer able to resist the temptation, Darcy lowered his head and kissed her.

When their lips touched, the heat in the room doubled. They grazed each other's mouth hungrily. He sucked her thick lips passionately before thrusting his tongue into her mouth, swirling it around inside before pulling out. Her tongue followed his action. When she pushed into his mouth, he sucked it hard.

She nearly came at that instant as she again remembered the incident when they had worked late in the laboratory.

What her mother didn't know was that Charles and Jane hadn't met through Longbourn Wishes. Elizabeth had introduced them because she worked for Dr. William Darcy at his research facility. And Charles was Darcy's best friend.

Darcy had questioned her abilities at first, not believing in her scientific mind because she was so young. However, after several months of working together, he seemed to be giving her fairer treatment, respecting her and asking for her opinion more and more often.

She noticed him gazing at her time and time, although she found him fascinating, she had never suspected anything untoward of him. Nevertheless, they enjoyed many inspiring chats about their research.

On the night when they both worked late, they were taking a break in his office when he suddenly admitted to her that he'd had the *hots* for her for a long time. He claimed that he wanted to date her and, more astonishingly still, that he intended eventually to marry her. She was amazed. She hadn't known for certain what her own feelings for him were, back then. But he kissed her ardently, she responded fervently, and they ended up making love, just like that, on his couch.

The morning after had been ugly. She overheard him advising Charles to cool off his relationship with Jane, because Jane was a gold digger. And a co-worker, George Wickham, had told Elizabeth that Dr. Darcy intended to sack her for improper conduct.

As a result, Elizabeth had a huge row with Darcy. Afterward, she stormed off and sent in her resignation via email. He trashed it and told others that she was simply on leave. Within two weeks, Charles had proposed to Jane, and it became apparent to Elizabeth that she had caught only the end of Charles's conversation. Darcy had been advising him that Jane's *mother* sounded like a gold digger, and had merely asked Charles to be certain that Jane accepted him because of her own feelings, not because she was being pushed to do so by her mother.

He also sent an email to Elizabeth, saying that Wickham had twisted his words. Darcy intended to sack Wickham, not her, because he had been caught selling research results to a competitor.

Elizabeth had wanted to apologise to Dr. Darcy afterwards. Indeed, she had needed to speak with him, but other matters had intervened, and she had been procrastinating, postponing the moment of truth for the past month.

But she couldn't stall that decision any longer. The dear old boy was lifting her out of the cake and all the way to the chesterfield sofa, without stopping the kiss. As soon as he finally came up for air, she took the first opportunity to tell him immediately, "I am pregnant."

He had been lowering his head to continue the kiss but stopped midway. His mouth gaped open, and he gasped. "We are going to have a baby?"

She nodded.

And he smiled. The brightest and biggest smile adorned his face, revealing his lovely dimples. Then he traced his knuckles tenderly along the line of her cheek. "Are you happy about it?"

She nodded again, returning his grin with a shy smile.

"When were you planning to tell me?"

"I have dialled the first few numbers of your mobile a thousand times. But I thought I should tell you face to face. And then I thought I should wait until there was no chance of a miscarriage before I told you. And then I thought..."

He lowered his head and gave her a tender, deep kiss that went on and on. He poured his heart and soul into it. "It's okay," he said simply when the kiss ended. "You've told me now."

"Then can we go on that date you wanted?" she asked. She was worried that he might mistake her meaning, and so she added quickly. "I'm saying this not because I know I'm going to have your baby, or because I wouldn't be able to cope with this pregnancy alone, I'm saying it because...well...for one thing, because I miss our chats terribly."

"A date? Actually, I'd rather we went straight to the marriage bit." He beamed at her. "Elizabeth, will you marry me? I've loved you for over a year now, almost from the very beginning when you started working for me. You're smart, and caring and considerate. I can't bear to live without you by my side."

"You love me?"

"Ardently and fervently."

"But we haven't even gone out on a date."

"True, but I already know that you love your tea with milk, your steak almost well done and your chocolate dark. Your favourite colour is yellow, and you hate G-strings."

"Hey! How did you know about the G-string thing?"

"Remember the wedding of Mr. and Mrs. Collins? After the reception, he got drunk and talked about asking his wife to wear a G-string for their wedding night."

"Gross!"

"I know. He said he was lucky that his wife wasn't like you. Although she said that she hated G-strings as much as you did, she agreed to wear one for their wedding night."

"Absolutely gross! He said this in front of everyone?"

"No, just Richard and me."

"Well, I met this Richard. He's a leering man."

"He's my cousin. He was probably just teasing you. I'm sure you can handle him. Please, Elizabeth, don't keep me in suspense. Will you marry me?"

"Although I haven't loved you as long as you have loved me, I will be happy to spend the rest of my life with you. But I want to wait until the baby is born before we get married."

"When did you realise you loved me?"

"When I found out about the baby. I wouldn't want to have just any man's baby. Only yours."

Darcy's heart melted on hearing such a declaration. Their lips touched and locked for a long time. When they separated, he asked, "But why wait?"

"I don't want people to think you asked me to marry you – or that I agreed to marry you – only because you knocked me up."

"I don't care what people think. It's our lives."

"Hush. Let's not talk about it right now. It's your birthday." She cradled his face in her hands and kissed him soundly. Then she stood up and sang a few slow songs, while swaying sexily for him.

He was mesmerised, not just by her body, but by her voice and the glow surrounding her. The velvety sounds soothed his soul.

She poured some champagne for him and fed him morsels of delicious food. Every time he wanted her to join him on the sofa, she evaded him. It was his treat, his birthday.

After almost half an hour, he managed to catch her. Once the fire was reignited, Darcy was unstoppable. He traced a line of tender kisses from her mouth, down her neck. Brushing aside the furry Santa outfit, he nipped and licked her soft skin on the chest. His hands were busy smoothing over her hips, kneading her butt through the lacy fabric of her panties. Then, suddenly, he stopped, stood up, and lifted her off her feet.

"Where are we going?" she asked, wrapping her arms around his neck.

"I promised I would make love to you on a proper bed from now on." He grinned, the intensity of his gaze heating her up. "So I'm taking you to bed."

When he walked out of the library and up the stairs, he caught the eyes of several people through the gap of a half-open door down the hall.

"Good night, Mrs. Reynolds. Good night Georgie!" he called out in cheery mood, and explained to a wide-eyed, flustered Elizabeth, "Georgie's my sister."

"Hey, isn't the Santa going to sing for us, too?" Richard called out as he threw the door open.

Mrs. Reynolds elbowed him in the stomach. Georgiana smacked him on the arm and said, "Happy birthday, William. Elizabeth, great to meet you. Have a good time."

Elizabeth waved a weak goodbye to the onlookers and buried her red face against Darcy's shoulder.

He felt no embarrassment at all. He was taking the mother of his child to bed, and he was determined to persuade her to marry him as soon as possible. He walked steadily, in a confident manner, like a proud peacock on display.

Our dear boy and his personal Santa didn't show up downstairs until Boxing Day. He then swept her off to Pisa on a 'scientific research tour' concerning Galileo. When they returned two weeks later, our dear old boy persuaded Elizabeth to move in with him at his Knightsbridge house, and also to return to work, albeit on a lightened schedule.

Right after their first ultrasound, Darcy finally convinced Elizabeth to marry him without further delay. They had a grand wedding at Rosings, much to Mrs. Bennet's satisfaction, even though the bride was big with child by then.

But where was the disapproving Lady Catherine de Bourgh? Ah, remember that this is not Miss Austen's story. Our Lady Catherine gave approval to Darcy's choice, with no regard to the lady's wealth or connections, as long as they truly loved each other. Her only disapproval was toward her other nephew, Richard, who made a mess of her library in order to house the birthday cake.

And did Elizabeth kick Charles's ass for his part in the Santa-in-the-cake saga? Well, no, but only because Charles redeemed himself by 'accidentally' directing his sister Caroline to Pemberley when she planned to surprise Darcy with her own sexy Santa gig. By the time an angry and frustrated Caroline arrived in Kent, our dear boy had taken Elizabeth to Italy.

And did Dr. Darcy keep his promise to make love to Elizabeth on proper beds only? Definitely not. Of their next two boys, one was conceived on the desk in his library in London, and the other by the pond at Pemberley.

*What if Mr. Darcy stayed in Longbourn?*

## Room 69

"Is there a five-star hotel around here?" Darcy asked.

The teenaged receptionist with spiky pink hair, and mouth and nose piercings, folded her arms and said, "There's one about a mile away. But with the SlagFest on, in Meryton, I doubt they have a free room."

*SlagFest? What the hell is that?* He wondered. "I see. Well, could you ring the hotel and check for me anyway?"

She shook her head. "Too late. It's one in the morning. Now, old man, do you want a room or not? If not, I'm going back to sleep."

Gritting his teeth, Darcy nodded. He'd had a shitty day. The plane had been delayed, his luggage was lost in transit, and then his hired car broke down, nearly three miles from his friend Charles Bingley's new country estate of Netherfield.

Despite the late hour, he had rung Charles to ask him to pick him up, but Charles wasn't answering the phone. Next, he tried the car rental company, but they couldn't help him either, due to a large number of emergencies in

Meryton. But they gave him directions for walking to Hotel Longbourn, which was much closer.

Darcy was not used to staying in three-stars hotels. Longbourn itself was quite homey, with old country charm and a warm fireplace. But the service he had received from the receptionist left a lot to be desired. And his room, when he reached it, was small and smelled of paint.

He turned down the bed sheet, walked into the bathroom and stripped off his clothes. A shower was what he needed. Then he would crawl into bed and seek the sweet oblivion of sleep. Tomorrow was bound to be better, wasn't it?

So decided, he stepped into the shower stall. After the relaxing shower, he tried to switch off the taps – or attempted to. The hot water tap was off, though reluctantly. But when he turned the cold water tap, it wouldn't move. Using both hands, he tried again, more forcefully – and the tap flew off the pipe altogether.

He gaped as water flew everywhere inside the bathroom, spewing wildly from where the tap had broken off. Icy cold water sent shivers down his body. His clothes, which he had draped over the towel rod, were now drenched, as was the lone towel.

Realising that it was useless to try to stop the water, he strode out to the bedroom and rang the reception.

"Yes?" the receptionist answered groggily after the seventh ring.

Something in him snapped, and he burst angrily, "I've never been in such a crappy hotel in my entire life!"

"Sorry, sir. What can I...?"

"The bloody water tap just flew off the pipe," he shouted. "Water is shooting everywhere, and my Armani suit – the only outfit I have with me until my blasted luggage is found – is ruined!"

"Oh my. Did Lydia put you in Room 69?"

Then the line was dead.

Darcy fumed. *How dare she cut me off?* He was about to ring again when he heard someone knocking on the door.

Stepping over the growing pool of water oozing through the bathroom door, he crossed the room and pulled the door to the hotel corridor open. He was prepared to bite the head off the teenage receptionist – but it wasn't her. Instead, he found himself gazing into the most amazing pair of green eyes he had ever seen.

When he saw that she was looking at him with her mouth slightly agape, he remembered that he was buck naked, with water dripping down his chest and thighs.

A shade of red spread from her face to her neck and down her lovely cleavage. She wore a loose green V-necked T-shirt and denim shorts, and she looked like a pocket Venus, with her voluptuous curves. He swallowed hard and felt a surge of arousal coming on.

She instantly noticed that, as well. Her eyes grew larger still, and she licked her lips nervously.

Darcy retreated just long enough to grab the bed sheet and cover his raging little man.

"I...I'm sorry," the woman said in a shaky voice. "Lydia shouldn't have put you in here. This room is still under renovation. You say the shower...?"

Darcy looked toward the soaked bathroom, which was rapidly taking on the appearance of a small lake. When he turned back, he caught her staring at his butt. Hastily, he pressed himself to the wall and nodded. "If you can just shift me to another room...?"

"I'm sorry, we're completely full. But I can fix the tap," she said, and ventured toward the bathroom.

He wrapped the bed sheet around his lower body and followed her as she ducked into the water-coated bathroom and, ignoring the shower stall, approached the sink vanity. Opened the doors of the cabinet, she got down on all fours and stuck her head under it.

He watched her in fascinated admiration as her bottom shifted forward and backward, right to left, and then left to right. *What is she doing under there?* He wondered. *There isn't any water leaking through, down there.*

"Damn! It's too tight for me to screw," she said, and backed out far enough to turn and look at him.

He gasped as he saw that her T-shirt, thoroughly wet from the bathroom spray, was stuck to her body, and that she didn't seem to be wearing a bra. Her nipples stood forth, hard and proud, putting on a wet T-shirt show for him.

"Can you help me switch off this main?" she asked, and her flushed cheeks indicated that she knew exactly what he was gazing at with such rapt attention.

Darcy looked at the soggy carpet, then at her tempting body. He wanted to refuse because by helping her, his only protection, the bed sheet, would become wet, as well.

"Are you *coming* or not?" she asked impatiently.

*Any moment now!* he thought despairingly. *I haven't gotten laid for far too many months.* He nearly spoke the words out loud. Instead, drawing a deep breath, he walked into the bathroom, crouched down beside her, and reached under the vanity to place his hand over hers on the stubborn main.

They both felt a jolt of electricity zip through their bodies as they turned the stubborn knob together. Finally, grudgingly, it began to move, and soon the water stopped spewing from the shower pipe.

The room was suddenly silent, except for their heavy breathing.

Darcy cleared his throat. "I'm sorry I yelled at you on the phone," he apologised, and gave her a shy smile. "I'm William Darcy. I had a massively bad day, and that burst water pipe was the last straw."

"Elizabeth Bennet. Don't mention it. It's our fault." And she returned his smile.

When they stood up, their wet garments did little to conceal the heightened state of their bodies. They stole shy, hungry glances at each other.

"You're...all wet," he stammered, and tried to secure the bed sheet more modestly in place over his lower body, but the weight of the water kept dragging it down.

"You can...use my room for the rest of the night. I'll stay in the reception room," she added quickly, not wanting him to misunderstand.

"Thank you," he said, and followed her meekly, half naked, still dripping, to her room.

The next morning, Mrs. Bennet followed the trail of water damage on the carpet. When she burst into her second daughter's room, she found Elizabeth snuggled tightly against a handsome, nude stranger.

Her screams could be heard as far as Netherfield.

Despite Elizabeth's insistence that nothing untoward had happened during the night, Mrs. Bennet was ecstatic about the event as soon as she learned that Mr. Darcy was worth billions.

When Darcy and Elizabeth got married, six months later, Mrs. Bennet took Lydia on a round-the-world holiday, as her reward for putting Mr. Darcy in Room 69.

*What if Mr. Darcy was an international movie star?*

## Something Fishy

BBC news: Nick Darcy, Britain's youngest Nobel Prize winner in medicine, was married today.

"How did you and your wife meet, Professor Darcy?"

"Well, she was originally my grad student. The first time we met, she asked me whether I had really been conceived in that fish tank," Nick said, and grinned.

Standing behind Professor Darcy were his proud parents, William and Elizabeth Darcy.

"So, was he, Mrs. Darcy?"

"You've been asking us this question for ages. You already know that I won't tell you," Elizabeth replied to the reporter, then winked at her husband of 32 years.

Yes, Britain's public all wanted to know about the truth about the most romantic and sizzling moment in the world's cinematic history.

William Darcy was smiling, too, obviously proud of his wife and three sons. He, too, found himself thinking back to that day in the fish tank....

*Thirty-two years ago*: Mr. William Darcy had been Britain's cinema heartthrob for some years and was getting more and more bored with the movies in which he had lately played. Then he met Elizabeth Bennet. She had already written three romance novels, and her latest one was going to be made into a movie by Bingley Production. She would be the on-set screenwriter. He had first met her nearly a year earlier, and was enchanted by her quirky humour, her gorgeous figure and her sparkling personality.

It was unfortunate that he had gotten off on the wrong foot with her, when she overheard him criticising her novels. He hadn't really meant it, as he hadn't even read them at that time. He had just been annoyed by his friend Bingley's constant badgering for him to take on this new movie.

Of course, after meeting Elizabeth and becoming familiar with her novels, he had signed on for the movie, despite the depressing fact that Director Hurst had cast his sister-in-law, Caroline, as the lead actress. Darcy wanted to spend more time with Elizabeth, even if that meant having to put up with Caroline Bingley.

In typical cinema fashion, the crew was preparing to shoot the final scene first. It would take place in a huge glass fish tank the size of a 20-foot container, located on a deserted beach. The tank was filled with gallons of water and tons of beautiful coral, to make it look as if he was deep-sea diving with Caroline. She would have problem with her oxygen tank, and Darcy's character would help her to the surface, whereupon they would make sensual love in the water, nude.

He didn't like the fact that the scene might fuel Caroline's imagination. She was shallow and mercenary, and he would never want her to be his girlfriend. But the script was sensational, and the extremely romantic scene would make a great end to the story. Hurst had also reassured him that it would be done tastefully, without full-frontal shots. Darcy had a feeling that the movie would be a hit. He wanted to play Elizabeth's hero and help to bring her talents the fame that they deserved.

On the initial day of the shoot, Caroline threw a fit, saying that the water in the fish tank was too dirty. She didn't want it touching her makeup, hair and skin. She demanded that the script be changed, or that the whole scene be relocated to a swimming pool. Since neither of those solutions could be adopted, for artistic and practical reasons, a stunt woman was summoned to stand in for Caroline.

But that didn't make Caroline happy, either. "Keep your hands and lips away from William during the shooting, or I'll make sure you aren't hired to work in this industry for the rest of your life," Caroline threatened Mary King, the stunt actress, before the screen diva stormed off to a nearby casino for a bit of rest and gaming.

Mary King, shaking with fear, started to experience an asthma attack immediately before she was scheduled to dive into the water to join Darcy.

Seething, Hurst looked around frantically for another replacement. He couldn't afford to postpone the scene, due to Darcy's busy schedule and the cost of the set. Finally, his gaze fell on the novelist. Elizabeth Bennet would do. She knew the script inside and out. Due to Caroline's breasts enhancement procedure, she and Elizabeth even shared similar voluptuous curves. The only difference was that Caroline was three or four inches taller than Elizabeth. Still, Hurst was confident that he could hide the height difference, since it was a water scene.

It took a bit of time and effort to persuade Elizabeth, as she didn't want to be nude in front of the cameras, especially in the company of the once-arrogant but lately rather polite actor who would be her co-star for the scene.

Finally, it was her sister Jane who managed to persuade her. Jane was the production assistant, and she knew the financial implications to Bingley Production if shooting had to be delayed for days because of Caroline's tantrum.

Darcy had continued to swim, inside the fish tank, after Caroline left, content to let all the drama play itself out without his involvement. He was trying to summon the proper mood so that he could act believably amorous with a stranger. Finally, as the delay dragged on, he indulged in imagining that he would be making love with Elizabeth.

When Elizabeth dove into the fish tank with a mask on and swam with him, he thought she was Mary King. He swam and acted according to the script's instructions and, when she acted distressed about her oxygen, placed his arm around her waist.

Suddenly, he felt her shiver.

Gazing intently through the dark water and obscuring masks at the woman beside him, he finally discovered that he was swimming with Elizabeth, not Mary King.

His mind blanked for a second. Then his pent-up emotions kicked in. Suddenly, he felt like he really was the hero of the movie, genuinely concerned over her difficulty. Pulling away her breathing tube, he pushed his own between her lips so that she could take a breath.

When she returned the tube, he found that he could discern the sweet taste of her on the mouth piece. Back and forth it went as they continued to share it for several minutes, as called for in Hurst's shooting directions.

All the while, he treasured the feeling of having her so near to him. He could feel his arousal mounting, despite the cool water temperature.

Slowly, they rose until they reached the surface, and he wasn't acting as he slowly took off her mask, threw it aside and held her face tenderly. In that moment, she was the most beautiful of women, in his eyes. He lowered his head and tasted her lush lips.

The kiss sizzled, conveying the passion that had built up within him over the past year. It also fit the movie so well that all four cameras continued to roll.

The script and reality seemed to merge in Darcy's head. Slowly, he pushed off her breathing apparatus, unzipped her wet suit, peeled it away and took off her red bikini. His hands and body shook with pleasure as he caressed her smooth skin.

Elizabeth was overwhelmed, as well. He had kissed her once, in Kent, when he asked her to spend a night with him. She had slapped him, then, for his arrogance...but she had still enjoyed the kiss.

This time was completely different. His lips seemed to ignite every inch of her body. His hands branded her skin. It didn't take a script to convince her to pull his wet suit and swimming trunks away, as well, her hands as frantically eager as his.

Soon, they were naked against each other, breasts against chest. She could feel his arousal, and she wrapped her legs around him, in a blending of instinct and script.

As they grasped each other's bottoms and moved against each other underwater, their heat, sensuality and love were captured on camera. They kissed and caressed each other passionately, above and beneath the water.

They were so involved with each other that they didn't even realise that the cameras had stopped and the crew members were packing up. Jane had to call out several times for them to stop.

They finally separated in the water and made their way to the side of the tank, where they grabbed towels and robes from Jane as they emerged. Then they bid her goodbye and drove away from the set at high speed.

The next day, Hurst had another drama on hand. When Caroline heard about the sizzling scene in the fish tank between Mr. Darcy and Miss Eliza, she threw another fit. She walked off the set altogether and refused to continue filming unless the script writer was taken off.

Since the movie was based on Elizabeth's novel and she retained the script adaptation rights, there was no way that Hurst could yield to Caroline's demand. And Hurst knew on-screen chemistry when he saw it. Instead of letting Caroline ruin the production, he persuaded Elizabeth to take over Caroline's role for the entire movie, instead.

Elizabeth was hesitant at first, as her only prior acting experience had been in high school. But, with the encouragement of Darcy and Jane, she finally agreed.

As a result, drama queen Caroline Bingley was kicked off the project altogether, even though she threatened to sue Bingley Production for breach of contract.

"Something Fishy" became the highest-grossing romantic comedy in box offices around the world. The five-minute-long above- and under-water love making scene was often voted as one of the most sizzling and beautiful moments in movie history.

After that, Elizabeth's novels topped the best-selling lists many times, but Mr. Darcy and she refused millions of dollars from producers around the world to act together on screen again.

In fact, Darcy quitted acting and took up directing instead. His movies were often box office hits and earned him several Academy Awards.

The couple married soon after the movie was completed, and Nick Darcy, their first son, was born exactly nine months to the day after the fish-tank filming.

That was why the media constantly questioned whether Darcy and Elizabeth had conceived their first baby in the fish tank, in front of cameras and, eventually, a worldwide audience.

What do you think?

Well, the author could tell you a secret. Nick was not conceived in the fish tank. But his parents were so eager for each other, after they emerged from the fish tank, that they didn't manage to drive the car all the way back to the hotel. Instead, they pulled over and parked on a quiet country lane, where they made mad love together in Darcy's car, to their mutual satisfaction.

*What if someone became jealous of Darcy and Elizabeth's romance?*

## The Condom Thief

"No self respecting man in the world will buy it for his woman!" Darcy protested heatedly.

"I'm not your woman! I'm your sweet sister, remember?" Georgiana said, reclining on the bed in a clean but simple room in a motel.

"Can't you wait? We'll get to Netherfield tomorrow."

"Do without? You must be joking! This is my first day. It is like the Red Sea flooding the beach. Anyway, Charles is not there, so we are stuck here. Just go and find a damn supermarket and stop arguing."

"What's wrong with the ones in the vending machine outside?"

"Those are tampons. I don't use tampons."

"But you don't even have an empty package to show me! How am I supposed to know what to buy?"

"Can't you read, Mr. Business Genius? It reads 'Stayfree Super Ultra Thins Cotton Soft with Wings.' Remember that! Don't buy the silky ones."

"Who on earth invented such a product with such a long name? And what's wrong with the silky type? I should think silk would be better than cotton."

"'Silky', not silk. It's synthetic, and I'm allergic to the silky type."

"It's too damn complicated," he groused. "Can't you just come and choose it yourself?"

"You got us lost in this goodness-knows-where little town because you were too stubborn to listen to my directions on the road. You lacked the sense to alert Charles that we're coming a few days early, so Charles is not there. So it is up to you to fix this. Go out and buy me some Stayfree. Now! I am in pain, I cannot move, and I need them tonight."

Darcy hung his head and stalked out of her room. Returning briefly to his own room, he collected his wallet, car keys and, most importantly, his sunglasses. He was absolutely going to need sunglasses when he went in to buy sanitary napkins.

When he rounded the corner of the corridor, after leaving his room, he bumped into a woman near the vending machine. She had long, curly, chocolate-coloured hair, and she wore a loose T-shirt and an old pair of jeans. The packages she had been holding dropped to the floor.

Darcy bent down to gather them for her, then hesitated in surprise as he saw three packs of condoms lying there. "Well prepared for a whole-night session?" he commented before he could think better of it.

"Not that it's any of your business, mister," She said angrily. She had sparkling eyes that enhanced the loveliness of her face, but her expression was not a happy one.

He recoiled, exasperated by her manner. Who was this woman, to get annoyed with him? After all, he hadn't bumped into her on purpose, and he had helped to pick up what she dropped. Fuelled by the frustration of the long day, he said, "Maybe you don't need much preparation. If he only needs small condoms, you may not even notice he's inside you."

"What! Can you get any cruder? I suppose, next, you're going to claim that you use extra-large ones. Every man loves to boast, especially your type!"

He didn't like her sarcastic tone. "And what would you know about my type? As a matter of fact, yes, I do use the extra-large ones, but why would I need to boast to you? When it comes to figures, Marilyn Monroe you're not."

"Oh my, I'm absolutely devastated, James Bond! Until I see for myself, every man is extra-small."

"Who is being the crude one now? We just met, and you want to see my extra-large? You must be deprived."

The woman glared at Darcy and snatched the condoms from him. "I wouldn't shag you even if you paid me, Mr. Jumbo!"

"Why would I need to pay you? I have heaps of Marilyn Monroes throwing themselves at me."

"And I have hundreds of James Bonds queuing up to bed me."

"I can make you beg, with just a kiss – and I won't need to spend a penny." Darcy said heatedly, and did the unthinkable – he kissed her, a perfect stranger, in a public place. He pressed her to the vending machine and kissed her hard on the mouth. Her lips were hot and wet, and her body proved not to be shapeless at all. In fact, he could feel her generous breasts pressing firmly against his chest. Her nipples hardened, grazing against his torso as she squirmed. He smoothed his hands over her hips, savouring her curves.

Darcy rubbed his body against hers, making her gasp for breath and moan out loud. When she parted her lips, he thrust his tongue inside. He tasted her eagerly for a lingering minute...and then she bit his tongue.

He yelped in pain and raised his head. "What was that for? You were moaning for more." Indeed, he could see that her eyes were still filled with desire.

"In your dreams!" She pushed him farther away, gathered the condoms that had fallen to the ground again during their kiss, and ran towards the back of the motel.

He touched his tongue. Luckily, there was no blood. He couldn't believe he had pounced on a stranger. He could be accused of assault. "Think of the scandal that could bring upon the business!"

He had not been exaggerating when he said that he had heaps of women throwing themselves at him. As a thirty-year-old young man who was tall, dark, single and a billionaire, he found that all sorts of women were interested in dating and bedding him. At fundraising dinners and business functions, young socialites, trashy celebrities and divorced women all flocked to him.

But he was not interested in them at all. When his mother died due to complications after Georgiana's birth, he had turned from a happy and cheerful thirteen-year-old to a shy and melancholy teenager, rarely at ease with strangers. He grew up to be a sober man, and a world of responsibility descended on his shoulders after his father passed away, shortly after Darcy's twenty-first birthday. He had dated and bedded women, during the ensuing years...but he could count them on the fingers of one hand. As a rule, he found sex without emotion too crude, and the experience thus far had never given him a sense of completeness. He couldn't begin to understand why this woman, of all people, had incited such sudden emotion and such a strong reaction in him.

Thoroughly shaken, he climbed into his silver-blue Bentley Continental GTC and roared off down the road to carry out Georgina's distasteful errand.

***

After half an hour of speeding around on country roads, he finally calmed himself enough to ring Georgiana and tell her that he would be back a bit later. Not surprisingly, it earned him another earful from her.

Soon thereafter, he stopped at the supermarket, which was in fact, a mere ten-minute drive from the motel.

The store was larger than he had expected. When he walked inside, he was certain that all eyes were upon him. There were several elderly women inside the store, engaged more in chatting than shopping. The girl at the cash register wore a low-cut, tight T-shirt that showcased her small breasts. She flashed him a big grin, batted her eyelashes, smoothed her red-highlighted brown hair and said, "Welcome!"

Luckily, Darcy had his sunglasses on, so the girl couldn't see him rolling his eyes. He gave her a curt nod and walked down the nearest aisle, searching. Finally, on the far side of the store, he stopped in the shampoo area, which was next to the shelf where the sanitary napkins and tampons were displayed.

Suddenly he felt something brush against his arm, and a husky voice said, "Hi, stranger. Can I help you?"

He turned and saw a teenage girl in a tight red Lycra top, short black leather mini-skirt and plenty of makeup, standing very close to him. She had fake blonde hair and looked a lot like the young cashier. The only difference was that she had enormous breasts, fully on display. She pouted her red lips, gave him a smile and a wink.

He shuddered and said, “That’s okay. I’m just browsing.”

“I can explain the different brands of shampoo for you, if you want, luv. This one is SunSilk. I use it myself. It makes my hair look very silky.” She smoothed her hand over her hair and swayed her hips at the same time.

Darcy shut his eyes and wished she would disappear. He just wanted to finish the embarrassing errand and get back to the motel. He couldn’t very well ask her to shut up so he put up a frosty mask and said in a cold voice, “I prefer to look at them myself, if you would excuse me.”

He saw that she was about to open her mouth to speak again, but the girl at the cash register called to her loudly, “Lydia, we need to go if you don’t want to miss the movie!”

Lydia glared and took another look at him. He gave her an even frostier look. She bit her lip, hesitated, but finally gave up and walked reluctantly back to the counter area. Darcy breathed a sigh of relief.

He moved quickly in front of the shelves full of sanitary napkins. “Stayfree, Stayfree, Stayfree. Yes, there it is. Damn, there are so many different ones. Cotton soft, no wings, no. Silky soft with wings, nah. Regular day use, non. Super but not ultra thins. Damn! To hell with them!” He grabbed one each, 8 packs in total and walked toward the cashier.

Before he could reach his destination, however, he bumped into someone again. He cursed his bad luck as the packages of sanitary napkins flew from his hands and dropped onto the floor.

Darcy crouched down to pick them up and saw some packs of condoms scattered with them. A sense of foreboding struck him and he raised his eyes. The “condom woman" from the motel was there!

"More condoms! 3 packs in half an hour!" Darcy eyes widened. His raised voice drew the attention of the elder women. They were gathering around him and the woman.

"3 packs in half an hour!" they said in unison.

"Elizabeth, who is this young man you are banging? A superman?" one of them inquired, and they burst into chuckles.

Darcy and Elizabeth blushed all red. She sorted out the condoms from among the sanitary napkins and stood up. He did the same. She glared at him, and then a wicked smile appeared on her face. Wrapped her arm around his waist, she said, "He's not a superman, Mrs. Short. Otherwise I would get the extra-large condoms, not the small ones. And we didn't use up 3 packs in half an hour. He's so nervous that he dropped them into the toilet bowl."

"What the ...?" He was about to protest and shake himself from her hold when she stood on tiptoe and shut him up with a kiss, right in front of the ladies.

"Where did you find this delicious young man?" Mrs. Short asked.

Darcy had enough of irritating women for one day. He was not about to become the subject of supermarket gossip. He managed, belatedly, to shake free from Elizabeth. Hastily, he scooped up the sanitary napkin packages and placed them on the counter.

The women burst into a flurry of comments. "Why does he need all these sanitary napkins, Elizabeth?" "Are they for you?" "How sweet!" "So the sex was interrupted because your period started?" "Why do you need the condoms then?" "I'm all confused now."

Darcy scowled. "Where the hell is the cashier? I want to pay and get back to the motel."

Elizabeth walked behind the counter, flashed him a grin, and said, "You can pay me, my dear! And I need more than a penny."

"So he was banging you at your motel?" "No wonder you were late! Lydia and Kitty had been complaining."

"Your motel?" Darcy asked.

"That will be £38.25."

"He didn't know your family owns the motel and the supermarket?" "How sweet. At least he wasn't shagging you for your money!" "But why come in, then? You have another three hours before closing time. He'll be all alone at the motel if you stay." "Yes, Lizzy, you go with your young man. I saw Mary at the back. I am sure she'll be willing to cover for you." "Mary! Come and say goodbye to Elizabeth's bonk buddy." "Yes, go back, have a cuddle and keep him warm" They then broke into giggles again.

As soon as Darcy and Elizabeth finished the transaction, they were hurried out of the store by the bevy of elderly women.

"Wow, he has such a sleek ride!" "Oh, he won't be after your money then, Lizzy." "Unless he's the car salesman." "Don't worry, young man, Elizabeth's no gold digger." "Yes, she won't sleep with you just because you are loaded." "She's the nice and honest one, nothing like Lydia." "You two should go parking in one of the country lanes." "Yes, all leather seats!" "I wished I were in my twenties." Another round of giggles was heard.

Before they could protest, Elizabeth buckled herself into the passenger side of Darcy's car. He thought it futile to argue and kick out Elizabeth, especially in front of their audience. Taking off his sunglasses, he started the engine and drove back toward the motel. But deep down inside, he was fuming.

"What the hell was that for, kissing me in front of everyone? Are you so sex starved in this small town that you had to grab the first stranger passing your way? And now they thought I was your "bonk buddy." Did you do that to improve your social standing in town? Were you as nice as they thought? I bet you weren't, otherwise, why would you be grabbing condoms every chance you have?" Darcy had never spoken so much, so fast and so angrily since his boyhood.

"Stop the car! I don't have to sit here and listen to your crap." When he ignored her and drove on, she smacked him on the arm and said, "If you don't stop the car now, I will pull the hand brake and skid the car."

"Damn!" He slammed on the brake, pulled it onto the shoulder of the road, unbuckled his seat belt, and turned to her, scowling. "Don't you dare do anything so stupid! My sister is waiting for me in the motel. I don't need your aggravation after what has been a very long day."

She unbuckled her seat belt, too, turned to face him. "You think that only you have had a long day! I'd just been mauled by a stranger in my own motel. And then you turned up to accuse me of being sex-starved and promiscuous. Well, I think you are the crazy one!" she snarled, and gave him a push

Fuelled by a haze of anger and sexual tension brought on by her kiss in the supermarket, he pushed her back, all the way against the leather seat, and crushed his lips to hers. She struggled for a few seconds, then yielded suddenly to his heat, wrapping her hands around his neck to pull him even closer. After a few minutes of hot kisses, he pressed a side button, and the seat reclined. He manoeuvred his position until he was over her, his weight pressing her body into the leather.

His hands were busy pushing up her baggy T-shirt, unclipping the front fastener of her bra, and fondling her firm breasts. Her skin was soft and smooth. His fingers squeezed the generous mounds, then rubbed and plucked at her nipples. He felt his blood pounding towards his lower body. He thrust his tongue into her mouth while he rubbed his arousal against her thighs. She put her hands under his shirt, exploring his muscular torso.

He stopped kissing her for a second and pressed another button, to switch on the car's dome light, and found that he was even more aroused by the picture she made in the dim light. Her curly brown hair was spread on the saffron seat. Her glittering eyes were filled with desire. Her lips were swollen from his kisses. Her baggy T-shirt was pushed right up, revealing breasts that were lush and nipples that were rosy. Her bra was not frilly but crisp and white.

Her belly was slightly rounded. He didn't like women too slim, as if they were dying of hunger. She had just the right amount of curves.

He couldn't help himself – he wanted to unwrap the whole of her. He unbuttoned her jeans and eased them down, exposing simple white panties that covered a triangle of dark hair dimly visible underneath. He lowered his head and pressed his nose to her triangle, breathing in the scent of lavender and sex.

He was about to push down her panties when the sound of a car speeding past broke his concentration. "This is crazy! I don't even know you, and I'm seducing you in my car." He pulled away from her, sat back in his seat and took deep breaths to calm himself.

"Ditto!" Her breathing was shallow and rapid. She sat up, as well, readjusted the seat. Using her fingers to tidy her hair, she then repositioned her clothes. After a moment of silence, they turned and looked at each other – and instead of getting angry, burst out laughing.

"I'm sorry for bumping into you and arguing so much, Elizabeth. My name is William Darcy. My sister Georgiana and I came to visit a friend at Netherfield, but we got lost and checked into your motel."

"I'm sorry to have taunted you, as well. I'm Elizabeth Bennet. I work in the family motel and supermarket. Just tell me one thing before we go any farther. Why did you buy so many different sanitary napkins?"

"Georgiana needs them. She's...you know...and she didn't feel up to going to the supermarket herself," Darcy said, and blushed.

"She needs eight different packs tonight?"

"She told me which one to buy, but I couldn't remember when I got so stressed out in the supermarket," he replied sheepishly. "Now it's your turn. Why did you have so many condoms, every time I bumped into you?"

"We have a condom thief here! I was doing a stock check at the motel, and then at the supermarket."

"A small condom thief?"

Elizabeth nodded, and they burst out laughing once again.

"So, how many condoms has the thief stolen?" Darcy asked.

"Five packs from the motel and ten from the supermarket," Elizabeth replied.

"How did you discover the theft?"

"One morning, about a week ago, I discovered that someone had tampered with the vending machine in the motel. Everything was accounted for except for five packs of small condoms. Then, the next day, when we were closing the supermarket, I found that the condom shelf was very untidy and appeared to have much less stock than the day before. I checked the sales report for the day and it didn't include any condom sales, so I did a stock check."

"But the condoms are quite close to the cash register. Surely one of your cashiers would have noticed the theft."

"You saw my sisters Lydia and Kitty, when you went in. They're not the most attentive staff."

"Lydia and Kitty... Those are your sisters?"

"Yes. Unfortunately, they spend more time flirting with the men who come into the supermarket than doing their job."

"Have you reported the thefts to the police?"

"It was just 15 packs of condoms. It may be a one-off - - well, a two-off – thing."

"You don't have a security camera?"

"Mary, my other sister, was supposed to make sure that the security camera was well maintained. Unfortunately, that didn't happen, either. She said she was busy catching up on her studies." Elizabeth grimaced and shrugged. "I guess I'm too slack with my staff."

But Darcy's mind was now focused on the mystery. "It has to be a guest staying at your motel. I don't believe a local could wander in without being noticed. After all, it's a small town. So, did any of the guests who've stayed at the motel during the past few days seem suspicious to you?"

Elizabeth considered the question. "Last week, our cousin, Pastor Collins, came to stay. Then the Bingleys. They had problem with a gas leak at Netherfield and had to spend two nights in the motel. There were two army officers, as well – Mr. Denny and Mr. Wickham."

Darcy straightened in surprise. "George Wickham?"

"You know him?"

"He's one of the worst characters I've met in my life, if we are talking about the same man."

"Really? He seemed quite charming, and he was very polite to everyone. Do you think he's capable of petty theft? I thought the army checked to be sure that officers didn't have a criminal record."

"Petty theft? I wouldn't know. The last I heard of him was about a year ago."

"What did he do then?"

As Darcy debated whether he should tell her, they arrived back at the motel.

"Lizzy! Who is this young man?" a plump, middle-aged woman squealed as Darcy and Elizabeth emerged from the Bentley. "Mrs. Short just called and said you were sleeping with a delicious young man all afternoon, here, and that's why you turned up late at the store. Is this he? Is this his car? He is not a car salesman, I hope?"

"Mr. Darcy, this is my mother," Elizabeth said, mortified by the woman's outburst. "Mom, Mr. Darcy is a guest here. Mrs. Short and the old ladies at the supermarket were just confused. Mr. Darcy, I won't delay you. I'm sure Georgiana is waiting for you."

But Mrs. Bennet was not about to give up so easily. "Tell me, Mr. Darcy, where did you come from? And who is 'Georgiana'?" She turned back to Elizabeth. "He's got a girlfriend already? Ah well. It had to be too good to be true. Jane's ten times prettier than you are. Should I ask Jane to relieve you at the reception desk?"

Darcy's eyes widened. How could her mother belittle her in front of a stranger! But Elizabeth seemed to take it well. She just rolled her eyes and signalled for him to go back to his room.

He nodded towards both women and made his way back to Georgiana's room. The explanation about Wickham would have to be postponed.

***

Darcy didn't see Elizabeth for the next two days, although Mrs. Bennet paraded all her other daughters in front of him as Georgiana and he ate their breakfast. Jane was a tall and very pretty blond, completely different from Elizabeth. She seemed very sensible when she spoke to them, but he found her too sweet and quiet. Anyway, she seemed to have met Bingley, and spoke shyly about how friendly Bingley was.

Mary was also blond, but her plain features gave her a rather dull appearance. Worse, she talked on and on about philosophy in a way that made her audience sleepy. The youngest girls, Kitty and Lydia, were both menaces. They liked to flirt, and they were silly in everything they said. He shuddered every time they spoke to him.

It became clear to Darcy that Mrs. Bennet was extremely annoyed with him. He heard her complaining to a friend on the phone that she couldn't understand why Jane's beauty and Lydia's fabulous body failed to tempt him. She even speculated that he must be gay.

Darcy felt for Elizabeth. She seemed to be the hardest-working person in the family. He often heard her mother and younger sisters saying that she was working at this and that, either at the supermarket or in the motel. Except for Jane, who worked on the family accounts, the Bennet women seemed to spend all of their time flirting, gossiping, daydreaming and painting their nails.

He was disappointed not to have a chance to say goodbye to Elizabeth before his move to Netherfield. And he didn't know whether to feel more relieved or worried that Bingley had invited the entire Bennet family to his housewarming party. Although Darcy didn't like socialising with strangers, he did want to have a chance to get to know Elizabeth better, and yet he shuddered as the thought of socialising with the other Bennets.

Bingley brought the elder Bennet sisters to the table where Darcy was sitting with his sister and Caroline Bingley. "Georgiana, Darcy, let me introduce you to Jane and Elizabeth Bennet. They work at the motel and supermarket in Meryton."

"Oh goodness, you're the 'condom woman'!'" Georgiana squealed.

"Hush, Georgie!" Darcy kicked her under the table.

"Damn!" Georgiana glared at him. "What was that for?"

"Condom woman?" Jane, Caroline and Bingley echoed in surprise.

"Yes, that's me," Elizabeth said, and smiled stiffly.

Georgiana had the good grace to blush. "Sorry for bursting out like that, Elizabeth. I'm pleased to meet you. My brother here hasn't been able to stop talking about you, these past few days."

"Hello, Elizabeth. Nice to see you again," Darcy said. His face was red, as well. Caroline's hand grasped his arm with force.

"So, what on earth is this 'condom woman' story?" Bingley asked.

Mrs. Short chose that moment to barge in. "Oh, Mr. Bingley, hello! You certainly host a wonderful party! Jane, dear, you look as gorgeous as usual. Elizabeth, I see that you are here with your bonk buddy!"

"Bonk buddy?" Georgiana, Jane, Caroline and Bingley exclaimed, looking from Elizabeth to Darcy in turn. The former was visibly flustered, while Darcy's face couldn't get any redder.

"I think I will go and get something to drink," Elizabeth murmured, and walked away.

Darcy jumped up, shook off Caroline's grasping hand, and followed Elizabeth, saying, "I'll help you." Caroline tried to stand and give chase but Bingley settled into Darcy's chair and grabbed his sister's hand. "Caroline, I need to ask you something ..."

As soon as they had a shred of privacy, Elizabeth said, "Sorry William. I shouldn't have joked about us in the supermarket. Mrs. Short and the other old ladies are gossip gurus. They forget, two minutes after they borrow ten dollars from you, but they can remember all the town gossip for years." Darcy and she got their drinks and moved to a secluded spot at the back of the garden.

"That's fine. I know I provoked you. You've been busy?"

She shrugged. "Sales in the supermarket are so-so. The motel is doing a bit better."

"Do you have a website for the motel?"

"I've been hoping to do that for ages, but I'm just too busy."

"Hertfordshire has a lot of green grounds for hiking and cycling. And your motel is in a very good location. I think, if you had a website for your motel, and some printed flyers for the supermarket in the motel to encourage more people to shop there, you could do pretty well."

"That's a very good idea."

"I can show you how to set up the website, if you want. I'm staying with Bingley for two months. I have plenty of time to spare." He smiled at her eagerly.

"You won't be golfing or partying?"

"I can do those things any time."

"And what would you want in return?" Elizabeth asked, and winked at him.

"Nothing." His smile had now become a grin, and he couldn't keep his eyes from her lovely face.

"You don't sound like a true businessman, with that attitude." She returned his smile.

They stayed with each other for the whole evening, moving from one spot to another to avoid Caroline and the gossiping grannies. Georgiana helped detain Caroline, too. By the time Elizabeth left at 2 a.m. with Jane, Darcy had extracted an "appointment" with Elizabeth for two days later, to teach her how to set up the website. He was also totally smitten by her wit, liveliness and dedication to her family.

***

"Thanks for coming again!" Elizabeth opened the door of her room in the motel, wearing a thin T-shirt with spaghetti straps and a pair of tight jeans. Darcy wished he could hug her as tightly as her clothes.

"Don't mention it," he said, and came inside the room for what was slated to be their third web design 'lesson.' Elizabeth's room was more of a studio apartment. She had an office area, a sitting area, an en-suite bathroom, and a tempting double bed.

"Do you want tea with milk again?"

"Yes, thank you."

"You go ahead and sit down. I'll be right there." When she came back with a cup of hot tea, she sat at his left, with her thigh touching his.

He felt a rush of heat, and forced himself to focus. "Well, we've already gone through most of the basics, and I've downloaded Joomla! onto your desktop. It's a content management system that's very easy to use. You'll find that they have a lot of templates to choose from, so you can select the colour and layout you like best."

"Wow, they look great."

"Yes. Why don't you show me a few of your favourite websites so that I can get ideas for the colour and layout. Maybe I can help you select the right template."

"Mmm... I love the look of the Forbidden Fantasy site. Let me find it for you on my 'Favourites' list." She leaned past him to grasp the mouse, and Darcy inhaled the faint lavender scent rising from her body. Her neck was right in front of his mouth, and he could see her cleavage when he looked over her shoulder. The creamy mounds inside her T-shirt were enticing, especially with her body dangerously close to falling onto his lap. He felt blood rioting through his body, especially after hearing her say 'forbidden fantasy.'

After a few mouse clicks, a dark, mysterious-looking website appeared on the computer monitor. It was like looking through a keyhole. He could make out a woman with dark, curly hair standing with her back towards him. She was almost completely naked, wearing only a black bra, matching G-string, and black fishnets hooked to a crimson garter belt.

His mouth felt dry.

Elizabeth clicked on the keyhole, and pictures of three different women appeared on the left side of the screen. The first image showed the front of a woman, revealing that her bra and G-string were, in fact, fashioned from fishnet too, except at the most important spots, where tiny, silky fabric cut-outs covered the strategic details. Next to this picture, the word 'Front' was spelled out in an artistic brush-stroke font.

The second picture showed a back view of the woman, in a slightly enlarged version of the picture from the website's homepage. The word 'Back' was written next to it.

The last picture made Darcy sweat. It showed the woman reclining on a bed with her thighs parted so that you could see the silky fabric of her G-string, with a few wisps of pubic hair clearly visible. Next to it appeared the word 'Open.'

"This is my favourite lingerie site," Elizabeth said, turning her head as she spoke to him. He could feel her breath. It smelled of chocolate. He was hypnotised by her red lips. He lowered his head involuntarily but, before he could kiss her, she turned back to look at the computer. "Let me show you the 'Open' section."

When she clicked the apex of the woman's thighs, another page appeared, displaying six photographs of different women wearing sexy and exotic underwear, lying on beds. The lingerie was presented in red, purple, cream, yellow, pink and green. The women had blonde, brown, red, black, silver and auburn hair, some straight, some curly, some long and some short. They posed with their thighs opened but in different ways, to show the different shapes of the silky fabric that cupped their womanhood and a variety of attached fishnets. Their hands caressed different parts of their bodies.

Darcy was sweating now because she had placed one hand on his thigh to support her weight as she leaned sideways to use the mouse. She turned her head again and said, "See the misty dark colour? And the fading edges of the photographs? I think it creates a very sexy, erotic message that urges customers to browse through the different pages and buy. Of course, I'm not saying it is suitable for our family motel. I just wanted to show you why I'd like to create the right atmosphere for my web page."

Darcy couldn't concentrate on her explanation. He was hot and aroused. He moved his body, pressing her against the computer desk, ready to kiss her. The mouse was accidentally knocked off from the table in the process, and she exclaimed, "Oh!"

She turned around again, effectively evading Darcy's lips as she rescued the mouse. But her incidental touch on the mouse activated a link. The computer screen changed, revealing an erotic page. Again, there were six photographs, but this time the photographs each featured a man and a woman, having sex in different positions.

Darcy groaned as he quickly glanced at the pictures. The first one was a man with his manhood thrust inside the woman from the back. The woman was bent over a table. In the next photo, the same man had the woman's legs over his shoulders while he was inside her. The woman was lying on the table. Following that, the next one showed the man lying on the table while the woman took his manhood in her mouth.

For the next three photographs, they were standing. In the first one, the woman was wrapped around the man like a little baby. The man was standing, buried deep inside her. The second picture showed the man licking the woman's sex while she leaned against a wall, eyes closed, legs opened. In the last photograph, the woman was standing near the table, with one leg on it while the man thrust into her from the side.

Darcy couldn't control himself. He wrapped his arms around Elizabeth's waist and lowered his mouth to her earlobe. "You're driving me crazy!" He felt her shiver as she turned around and replied, "Hey, I didn't do that on purpose. I really do like the design..."

He gave her a wet kiss, cutting off her words, then pulled her to sit on his lap. When he fondled her breasts through her thin T-shirt and bra, she squirmed, not seeming to realize that, by doing so, she was rubbing her bottom against his arousal, making it as hard as a rock. He trailed his kisses from her lips down her neck, from there to her shoulder, and finally came to rest on her breasts. He pushed the spaghetti strings off her shoulders and eased her strapless bra down to expose her hardened nipples to his hungry gaze.

He laved and sucked one nipple while he squeezed the other peak. His free hand travelled down, as if of its own accord, to cup her sex. But her jeans were too thick to give him a sense of the sweet body they covered.

He stood up, not removing his mouth from her nipple, and carried her to the tempting double bed. Once he had laid her down on it, he removed her T-shirt and jeans.

"Oh! You're wearing the Forbidden Fantasy!" Her bra, now pushed down below her nipples, was deep red. The cup was fashioned from a silky fabric in the shape of a tiny leaf, while the remainder of the bra was made of a fishnet material. Her matching G-string was also fishnet, and the silky fabric covering her mound was shaped like a heart. How Darcy wanted to kiss her heart!

Silently, she held out her hands to him.

Overcome, he tore the bra and G-string off her body easily, then lowered himself onto her.

"Hey!" She protested. "That was my favourite underwear!"

"We can browse and buy more after I taste all of you." He pressed hot, wet kisses all over her body. His mouth couldn't get enough of her twin peaks, while his fingers rubbed and slid along her folds. He used his other hand to free his manhood and was moving to pose himself at her entrance when she said, "Protection!"

"Damn! I don't have any with me."

"That's okay. I have some of those small ones from the last stock check, in the nightstand drawer."

Darcy laughed and wrapped her hand around his hard erection, "Do you think a small condom will fit?"

She traced her fingers over his thick, long manhood, then raised her head to have a look. Her eyes widened. "Clearly not. In fact, it may not fit into me, either!"

"Do you sell extra-large ones in the vending machine outside?"

"Yes."

"Then don't move! I'll be right back." Darcy pulled up his shorts, although he realised that it did little to hide his huge erection.

Elizabeth blushed. "Mom or one of the girls will see you. Let me go out to get it."

"Do you promise you'll come back immediately?" He asked, and collapsed onto the bed, cursing himself for not being more prepared. But he hadn't wanted her to think he wanted to spend time with her only on the chance that he could get into her pants, so he hadn't brought any protection.

"I promise." Elizabeth calmed herself, pulled her clothes quickly on again, and picked up her keys.

Less than two minutes later, he heard her shriek. Thankful that his arousal was no longer quite so obvious, he jumped out of the bed and rushed out of the room to check on her.

"The condom thief has struck again!" she said.

Darcy saw that the vending machine had been forced open, and several packs of condoms were scattered on the ground.

"Are you hurt?" Darcy asked, taking Elizabeth's hand.

"No, I'm fine."

"Do you need to report the incident to the police? I can go to the station with you."

"No, it's fine. Can you just gather up the condoms and tampons and put them in my room, while I will put an 'Out of Order' sign on the vending machine?"

"Of course."

Once he had done as she requested, he paced inside her room, unsure whether he should stay or go. He wanted to be with her, especially if she needed help. But he didn't want her to think that he had only lingered because he wanted to have sex. As he paced, he glanced at the computer from time to time. The porn page was still up. Should he turn it off?

Elizabeth came in, shut the door, and threw herself onto the bed, clearly deep in thought.

He knelt by the bed and took her hand. "You're sure you aren't hurt?"

"No, I'm fine. Just thinking," she said without looking at him.

"Do you want me to get you something to drink? Maybe a glass of wine?"

She turned to look at him and smiled. "Nurse Darcy, eh?"

Her smile was enough to lessen Darcy's worries. He returned the smile and said, "Only a nurse? No, I'd much rather be your doctor."

"Arrogant man! Nurses are more hard-working than doctors."

"Miss Bennet, do you want me to examine you, or do you want me to leave you to rest?" he asked, leaving the decision to her.

"You have to earn your keep! You can't leave your patient without an examination." Her eyes glittered as she moved farther onto the bed, draping one hand across her forehead and the other under her left breast. Then she said dramatically, "Oh, Doctor Darcy, I'm in pain!"

He couldn't help grinning, but he tried to speak in a sober, official tone. "Well, now, Miss Bennet, where do you feel the pain?"

"My heart." She then massaged the underside of her left breast in a slow, erotic way while she peeked at him from beneath her lashes.

Darcy swallowed. He could feel the blood cruising down his body again, but he continued in a formal tone. "Besides your heart, are you in discomfort anywhere else?"

"My legs, too."

"Which part of your legs?"

Elizabeth lowered the hand from the forehead and traced it slowly down in a path from her breast to her belly and onward until it rested on the apex of her legs. All the while, she kept massaging the underside of her breast with the other hand.

"There." She touched her inner thigh. "Right there."

He swallowed harder. "Let me get my equipment." Going to the coffee table, he sorted quickly through the condoms. Small... Medium... Medium... Large... Small... Finally, the Extra-Large! Placing the package on her bedside table, he said, "This sounds serious – heart *and* leg pain. Miss Bennet, please remove your clothes. I'll need to conduct a thorough examination."

She looked up at him.

He returned her gaze with a challenging glare.

"Yes, Doctor, of course," she said docilely. Sitting up, she pulled the tight top over her head, her breasts jutting with the action. Darcy remembered that he had torn her bra and underpants, and so she was naked under her T-shirt and jeans.

His arousal returned in full force.

She maintained eye contact with him as she lowered herself onto the bed and unbuttoned her jeans. Pushing them down slightly, she said, "Oh, Doctor Darcy, I'm afraid my jeans seem to be stuck. Could you please help me remove them?"

He considered the situation. Did she want him to be near her so that she could topple him onto the bed? He was enjoying her striptease and didn't want to abandon the view and join her just yet. Instead, he walked to the end of the bed, Aware that her eyes were focused on the outline of the rampant erection which was barely confined with his shorts.

Reaching the footboard, he put out his hands and tugged slowly at the bottom hem of her jeans. He couldn't look away as her womanhood was revealed, inch by breath-taking inch. He stopped when the waist of the jeans was pulled down to a point just below her knees, the stiff denim restricting her movements.

"Let me examine your legs first." He parted her thighs as far as the jeans would allow and knelt beside her, below her V. "Do you feel any pain here?" he asked, pinched her left thigh just above the knee up.

She shook her head.

"How about here?" he asked, moving several inches closer to her apex.

She bit her lower lip and nodded.

"And here?" he asked, moving closer still, his knuckles just brushing against her private curls.

"Yes!" she gasped. By now, Elizabeth's eyes were half closed, and she was using both hands to caress her breasts.

Savouring the sight of her pleasuring herself, Darcy pinched her folds and asked, "Do you feel any pain here?"

"Yesss!" she groaned.

He feasted his gaze on her sex. "Actually, Miss Bennet, I'm not surprised. This area looks decidedly swollen. Let me see if I can discover what the problem is." Slipping his hand between her folds, he discovered that her body was already hot and slick, ready to welcome him. Slowly, he pushed one finger into her.

Her breathing became shallow.

He slid a second finger in to join the first. When her breathing quickened, he began slipping them in and out, slowly at first, then faster and faster.

Elizabeth's hips moved as she bucked her body up and down to match his rhythm. Her hands abandoned the breasts, squeezing fistfuls of the bed sheet as she began to pant. Unable to resist the delectable picture she made, Darcy lowered his head and leaned down to lick and probe her wet folds with his tongue.

The intimate contact wrung a cry from her.

Emboldened, he applied himself with a will. In less than a minute, she reached a climax, writhing beneath his touch, then subsided, her face flushed.

"Well, Miss Bennet, I am concerned. You seem to be in a great deal of pain. I will need to examine you more thoroughly, with another piece of equipment." Hastily, he tugged her jeans all the way off, and stretched out beside her.

She turned, looked at him with a lazy satisfied smile that melted into a playful look of mock-concern. "But Doctor Darcy, you are not wearing your uniform. Let me help you change."

She tugged his T-shirt out of his shorts and over his head, then placed her small hands on his naked torso and said, "Much better. This is a very nice uniform!"

Impatient for her, he unbuttoned his shorts and pushed them off, so that he was as bare as she was.

"Now, let me prepare for a proper examination." He opened the condom package, tore one out and rolled it on, while Elizabeth stayed busy, rubbing her hands over his upper body.

When he turned to give her a kiss on the lips, she pulled back. "I didn't say I had pain in the mouth, Doctor Darcy. So what was *that* for?"

"A control experiment," he replied soberly. "I need to assess how deep the probing needs to go, between your legs."

"That's ridic..."

He lowered his head and kissed her again, cutting off her reply. Rolling on top of her body, he enjoyed her softness and her hard nipples as she opened her thighs, welcoming him. After several minutes of kissing her lips while he squeezed and massaged her breasts, he positioned his massive manhood against her wet entrance.

Finding her very tight, despite her recent climax, he said, "Deep breaths, Miss Bennet. This treatment is highly effective, if you relax and allow it to proceed."

"Yes, Doctor." She raised her legs and wrapped them around his waist, which elevated her body slightly and provided him with a better angle of penetration. Slowly, inexorably, he pushed inward until he could go no farther.

The sensation of her tight muscles clasped around his cock was exquisite. "Excellent," he murmured. "I do believe you're ready for the next stage of the treatment." After giving her a long moment to adjust, he began establishing a rhythm, thrusting in and out. As he began to move faster and faster, she scratched at his back, digging her fingernails into the muscles of his back. Then her hands slid down to his bottom, clenching there as her moans became louder and louder, rising until she screamed and reached another climax. Her inner muscles squeezed his manhood insistently, pulsing tightly. After a final flurry of thrusts, he surrendered, crying out her name as he erupted.

It took several minutes before Darcy had the strength to roll onto his back, bringing Elizabeth's body along and settling her on top of him. He caressed her face, her shoulders, her back, and then said, "So...do you approve of your doctor's bedside manner?"

Her eyes were still closed, but a broad smile curved her lips. "Your examination was very in depth, and your treatment for pain relief was absolutely fabulous. I'm much more comfortable now. But you never know. The pain might return in a few minutes."

"A few minutes? So quickly! I'll have to adopt a more aggressive treatment plan then."

"More aggressive? Is that possible, Doctor? I'm all ears!"

"I am confident of it, Miss Bennet – but some additional research into the latest studies may be in order for such an acute case. Perhaps we should continue our website design lesson. We need to replace your Forbidden Fantasy underwear, and I am sure we can find some ideas for improving my treatment plan if we take the time to browse through some of the more interesting links on the FF site."

Throughout the night, they surfed the web and talked. Darcy explained to Elizabeth that Wickham was a lowlife who liked to seduce young girls who had money. Wickham's father had been the business partner of Darcy's father, and Darcy and Wickham used to play together when they were young. Unfortunately, Wickham's father made a series of bad business decisions that caused him to go bankrupt when Wickham was fifteen years old. Darcy had lost touch with him, long ago. Then, a year ago, Wickham met Georgiana when she attended a summer camp in Ramsgate. He tried to charm her and conned some money from her, but Georgiana was quite streetwise and had alerted Darcy about it. The two of them had sent Wickham packing, not long afterwards.

Darcy and Elizabeth made love many times, that night, finally drifting off to sleep in the early hours of the morning. As a result, when there was heavy pounding on the door, neither of them responded to the noise.

The people on the other side of the door were too impatient to wait, so they turned the knob and, discovering that the door was not locked, barged inside.

"Elizabeth, you were supposed to relieve me at the reception!" Lydia complained petulantly.

"Oh my! You two raided the vending machine!" Mrs. Bennet cried out.

"Wow! Four packs of condoms opened, and seven used!" Mrs. Short exclaimed.

This last utterance woke the sleeping couple completely. Darcy was lying half on top of Elizabeth, with one hand on her breast and one leg tangled with hers. The sheet was barely covering part of their lower bodies, and he hastily pulled the sheet up to cover them both.

It was Jane who salvaged the situation. “Mom, Mrs. Short and Lydia, let’s talk at reception,” she said, and herded the other three women out of the room, with her highly developed diplomatic skills. Before she left, she winked at Darcy and her sister over her shoulder and said, “Lizzy, I thought you said he was only coming to teach you how to develop a website for our motel! Very nice development indeed.”

Elizabeth groaned and hid her face on Darcy’s shoulders.

Although Darcy had never been so embarrassed in his life, he was definitely happy to be waking up with Elizabeth. With a groan, he said, “Did we really use seven condoms? Who knew that old Mrs. Short would have such good eyesight?”

She turned to look over the edge of the bed at the condom packages and used condoms scattered on the floor. “Yes, it looks like she was spot on. Four packs and seven used condoms.”

“Yes, but you were just fooling around with the other sizes. You tried to use the small, medium and large condoms on me, and they didn’t fit.”

“Still, four times in one night is a record for me.”

“Me, too!” He pulled her back from the edge and cuddled her against him. “Do you suppose we have time for another round?”

“I’m afraid not. In fact, I’ll have to ask you to let me shower first. Then I’ll ask Jane to relieve Lydia. You and I need to go catch the condom thief!”

“How? Can’t we just forget about the thief? And wouldn’t it be more efficient if I join you in the shower? I could scrub your back. Or your front!”

“Sold!” Elizabeth gave him a kiss and pulled him along into the shower. Once the warm water was jetting against their bodies, she indulged in another round with him. He braced her hands against the cold tile wall, then bent her body forward and pumped into her from the back, again and again, proving to both of their satisfaction that practice did indeed make perfect.

"You have no problem with your mom and the others?" Darcy asked dubiously.

"Well, Jane's an angel. I don't know how she managed it, but she has shoved all of the rest of them out of the motel, and she's already handling the reception desk."

"Bingley called her that, too – an angel. So, where do you want me to take you? The police station?"

"No, to Netherfield. I have to see Charles."

"What does Charles have to do with the condom thief?"

"Be patient! I'll tell Charles and you together."

When they arrived at Netherfield, only Bingley and Mrs. Hurst were there. Darcy and Elizabeth lost no time pulling Bingley into the study, where Elizabeth said, "Charles, do you know why William called me the 'condom woman'?"

"Actually, yes. He told me about the condom thief."

"Well, last night I came face to face with the thief."

Both men stared at her, and Darcy exclaimed, "Elizabeth! You didn't tell me that you saw the thief last night. Was he armed?"

"It was a she, not a 'he'," she said, and turned to Bingley. "To be blunt, it was your sister, Caroline."

"What? Why would Caroline have to steal condoms?"

"I don't know. I only know that I saw her picking up some condoms from where the vending machine had been vandalised, last night. When I screamed, she ran off immediately. Do you want to talk to her about it?"

"She's gone shopping with Georgiana." He shook his head in bewilderment. "But why would she do such a thing? She has all the money in the world."

Darcy said, "Charles, if you and Louisa are willing, maybe the two of you could check Caroline's room for the stolen goods. They were all...ahem...in small size."

Bingley debated for a few moments, then left the study. When he returned, with Louisa in tow, he nodded his head and said, "We found twelve packs in her room. Some of them were opened, and the condoms had been cut into strips."

Elizabeth said, "I won't report this to the police, since they aren't a high-value item. But I think you need to talk seriously to Caroline about what has been happening."

Caroline at first denied the whole thing when her siblings confronted her. She claimed heatedly that someone else had planted the condoms in her room. However, after nearly an hour of reasoning with her, Charles and Louisa managed to break her down.

Tearfully, she explained that she had started stealing small condoms when she was fifteen. She had arranged a rendezvous with the school's soccer star, Mark, at a motel. When things got heated between them, he'd gone out of the room to get a condom...but ran into Daisy, Caroline's arch-rival from school, as he was making the purchase. Both girls had been vying for Mark's attention for months. Daisy normally had the upper hand, and when Daisy overheard Mark accepting Caroline's invite, she booked into the same motel to wait for her chance. When Mark came out of the motel room to buy the condoms, Daisy waited him to finish the purchase, then invited him to sleep with her instead.

Caroline waited for a while, but when there was no sign of Mark returning, she came out of her room, just in time to catch Mark and Daisy going into Daisy's room.

All hell broke loose. Caroline scratched and hit Daisy. Mark tried to separate the girls. In the end, he managed to shove Caroline to the ground, outside the room. Mark and Daisy then locked themselves inside. Caroline pounded on the door for almost an hour but they ignored her, and the loud sounds of them having sex were clearly audible through the door.

After an hour, Caroline's hands were bruised and swollen. Hysterical, she admitted defeat and turned to storm back to her own room, only to stumble upon a package of small condoms on the ground – the package that Mark had just bought.

Caroline became even more furious, imagining Daisy and Mark having sex without a condom, or the two of them having sex with a supply of condoms that Daisy bought. Fuming, Caroline retreated to her room, took a pair of scissors, and cut the condoms into strips. She felt much happier after that, so she went out to the vending machine, forced it open and supplied herself with a few more packages of small condoms to destroy.

That was the beginning of her compulsive behaviour. Every time she was sexually frustrated, she felt compelled to steal and cut up condoms.

What set off her thefts in Meryton?

Caroline had harboured hopes of seducing Darcy while he was staying under their roof at Netherfield, that week, but then he amended his plans and didn't come with them. When the gas leak forced the Bingleys to stay at the motel for two nights, the vending machine was too handy a temptation for a sexually frustrated Caroline to resist. And after the motel, she couldn't stop herself when she saw more condoms on display at the supermarket.

When Darcy went to teach Elizabeth web design, Carolyn followed, parking her car a short distance away and sneaking into the motel when no one was watching. She was jealous of Elizabeth, after meeting her at the housewarming party. The first two times that Darcy visited Elizabeth, he left after staying for an hour. The last time, however, he was inside Elizabeth's room for ages. Caroline crept up, when she was sure no one in the motel was looking, and eavesdropped on them. What she heard caused her to see red, and her compulsive urge to steal reappeared immediately, continuing until she was caught in the act by Elizabeth.

Deeply concerned, Charles took Caroline back to London and placed her in therapy.

So how did Darcy and Elizabeth's romance go, after that? Let's just say that he became adept at buying sanitary napkins for her, and she returned the favour by always buying the right-sized condoms for him.

*What if Darcy wanted to buy off Lizzy?*

## Best Hamburger in Town

"This is it?" Darcy asked Bingley with a touch of disbelief, wrinkling his nose at the sight of the dark, dull diner.

His friend nodded eagerly. "Out of our survey of 1,000 people, this place was voted to have the BEST hamburger."

The place was certainly busy. The two men waited for nearly 45 minutes before they received their burgers. Darcy had ordered one with lettuce, bacon, tomato, onion, cheese and mustard, while Charles went for pickles and relish in additional to the traditional filling.

After one bite, Darcy's eyes widened. It was hot, juicy and delicious. He pushed through the crowd and demanded to see the chef.

"You can talk to me, hunk," purred a young girl with a low-cut tank top, as she leaned her huge breasts against him.

He scowled and slipped a fifty-dollar bill to her. "I need to see the chef, now!"

"You're cute, but so beat." The girl pushed the note down her cleavage, then yelled at the top of her voice, "Lizzy, come out! Dad is here." Then she whispered to Darcy, batting her eyes, "Give me another hundred and I'll cover for her. That way, you can talk to her at the pub around the corner."

Darcy's lips tightened obstinately, but Charles took out the money and gave it to the young girl.

A minute later, 'Lizzy' came out. "Where's Dad?" she asked, looking around in confusion.

"This old chap needs to see you, immediately!" the young girl said, and pointed at Darcy. "I'll cover for you for an hour."

"Lydia!" Lizzy threw up her hands. "How many times do I have to tell you not to disturb me during my shift, especially with strange requests?"

But Lydia pushed Lizzy through the crowd and out the door of the diner, saying, "Just talk to them, or they'll kill me!"

"What? Why?" Lizzy sputtered, but Lydia had already retreated. Bewildered, Lizzy turned to look at the two men.

"Nice to meet you, Lizzy. I'm Charles Bingley from Darcy Production, and this is our president, William Darcy." He held out his hand, but Lizzy ignored him and turned to walk back into the diner.

"Hey, young lady, not so fast!" Darcy blocked her entrance. "We just want to know who the real chef is at Longbourn Hamburger."

Lizzy glared at him. "Move out of my way or else..."

Her flashing eyes made his heart jump. She might be young, but the stubborn set of her jaw held a certain allure. "I just want to talk to the chef. I'm producing a TV show. I want to feature Longbourn Hamburger. I'll make the chef a celebrity. He won't need to be stuck in this little hole for one more day."

"Is that right? How exciting!" Lizzy said cheerfully. "Come inside with me, and I'll show you."

Darcy felt a flood of warmth in his body when he saw her beautiful smile. He couldn't resist putting his hand on the base of her back, to guide her forward. The electric touch that resulted goaded him to do something he would never have done in normal circumstances. Bending toward her, he whispered in her ear, "Care to show me the, uhm, town's sight afterwards? I'd love to come with you."

Lizzy stopped dead and looked up at him, her mouth opening in astonishment. Her lips were just inches away from his, and he was tempted to kiss her there and then. But she moved away and walked into the diner with quick strides.

Two steps into the diner, Darcy saw a sausage flying his way. As if in slow motion, he saw it strike his chest, and followed the red and yellow stains of the ketchup and mustard smear that it left down the front of his Armani suit.

With two stomping steps, Lizzy returned to stand in front of him, glaring. "My name is Elizabeth Bennet, and I am the chef and owner of Longbourn Hamburger. And I would consider it a privilege to be 'stuck' in this so-called 'hole' for the rest of my life, Mr. hot-shot-celebrity Darcy!"

Then she leaned toward him on tiptoe, as if intending to give him a peck on the cheek. Whispering 'Enjoy the sights -- alone!', she slipped her hand beneath his suit jacket and across his torso, making him shiver. Then, before he quite realised what was happening, she slipped an egg into the breast pocket of his shirt, withdrew her hand, and patted him hard enough on the chest to break the egg.

When he swore in surprise, she arched her eyebrows, gave him a sweet smile and walked back into the kitchen.

*What if Darcy and Elizabeth hooked up, literally?*

## Can We Do It on the Street?

Darcy felt people pressing against him on all sides in the tube. With his height, he could look down at them, and he discovered to his usual exasperation that they were mostly women.

He cursed his cousin Richard for coming up with this month's team challenge: "Save the planet, take the tube." Darcy had been dutifully taking the underground for the past four days. He didn't know whether women recognised him or just liked his body so much that they took every chance to press against him, inside the underground.

However, when he felt a caress on his butt, he decided that enough was enough. Forcefully, he shoved his way toward a different part of the carriage.

A sudden lunge of the train sent him staggering forward, causing him to accidentally press a person hard against the door.

It turned out to be a woman with excessive curves. "Sorry," Darcy mumbled.

The woman looked up at him and, surprisingly, turned her body sideways so that they were not pressed against each other front to front. Instead of snarling at him, she simply acknowledged his apology with a nod of her head.

He breathed a sigh of relief. At least there was *one* woman who wasn't intent on taking advantage of him in the crowded underground. She wasn't extremely pretty but she smelled refreshingly of lavender, and her rich chestnut curls looked great. He was tired of women who dyed their hair blonde and copied celebrity styles. This woman, by contrast, was wearing a frilly, exotic dress with a matching shoulder bag, like an ethnic minority from Asia.

While he felt the accidental bumping and caresses at his back again, the woman at his front turned slightly, produced a mobile phone from her shoulder bag, and answered it.

"You don't want to know," she said, lowering her voice. She had a sweet voice. "Okay, you asked for it. Mom has set me up with a blind date... Yeah, I know... No, I tried to get out of it, but... Yes, I told her I had a group of Sri Lankans visiting, but you know my mother... He's called William..." She burst out laughing, causing a subtle wave of contact against his body.

"Told me his mom named him after William the Conqueror but he had no clue about his namesake...Oh, but he bragged about having a £50,000 chimney...and a £30,000 stainless kitchen...and a £10,000 four-poster bed...Yeah I know...failed miserably on my rating scale."

She indulged in another lovely round of genuine laughter. Most women he knew only pretended to smile seductively. They didn't seem to know how to laugh anymore. He found himself regretting that another man with the same first name as his had made such a bad impression on her.

"He wasn't bad looking. I'd give him a six on looks, but a two on ego, and barely a one on intelligence... Yeah... I know...you measure men's handsomeness by their wallet and I measure it by their IQ."

Darcy was sorry to see that the train had reached Knightsbridge. He would have been interested in hearing more about how she rated men. As the door opened, he walked out...but felt a certain pull on his body.

"Urgh!" The woman raised her voice, still pressed against him.

More people rushed out of the train, and Darcy and this woman were pushed forward.

"Hey, it's not my station yet!" she protested.

He didn't understand why she felt the need to tell him that. It wasn't as if he was making her leave the train. He started to walk on, and again she yelled out "Urgh!", her body still pressed against him.

His surprise edged toward annoyance. *Did she just lie to her friend about not judging a man by his wallet? Does she know who I am?* "What do you think you're doing, miss?" he demanded in a low growl. "I've had quite enough of being fondled by women on a train. Get away from me now!"

She looked up at him, revealing a pair of amazingly sparkling green eyes. *What a pity she's another fawning female!*

"Me?" she snapped. "Fondling you? Your ego is larger than the whole of England! See here!" She pointed to her chest.

*What a pair of gorgeous breasts – creamy skin, bouncy, and pushing tight against the modest bodice of that frilly dress. What a pity she's such a desperate woman that she'd try to preposition me right here in public!*

"Stop ogling and look where I'm pointing! Your shirt button is caught on my dress!"

"Oh!" As he diverted his glance from her lovely breasts and finally understood her point, his face turned bright red. "My word. I'm sorry!"

She put the mobile phone back into her shoulder bag and used her tiny hand to try to untangle the snag. She turned slightly, left and then right, moving her body up and down a bit, but it was no use.

Darcy was extremely uncomfortable. He felt sweaty with her touching his body like this in a public place, and he couldn't help noticing that some people waiting for the next train had begun to look at them strangely.

"Maybe we should do this at my place," he murmured.

Her hand froze, and she looked at him again with wide eyes.

"I mean...people are looking. Unless you have a scissor in your bag to cut it...?"

"No way! A Burmese refugee made this dress for me. I don't want to tear it."

"All right, you can take it off at my place, instead." Then his face turned a vivid red again, as he considered the words that he had just uttered.

"Are you a pervert?" she asked sharply.

"No! Not at all. I mean...my sister lives with me. She can lend you something to wear."

"That's an idea. But it might be better if we undress you, instead."

He gasped at her words, flustered and aroused as she tried to unbutton the offending shirt button. More people seemed to have gathered to look at them.

"Let's get out of here." He wrapped his arm around her waist and propelled her to walk along with him.

"Damn, it's no use," she swore. "Just stop. I can't do it when you're moving."

"I don't want to provide entertainment for the people here," he said.

She looked around. "Alright, then, we can do it on the street." She walked willingly by his side, like two lovers snuggled together for a romantic walk.

"You want to do it on the busy streets of Knightsbridge?"

She burst out laughing. "We sound like we're talking about having sex in a public place," She explained, and her face turned a shade of red.

*What a lovely surprise*. The women he knew had long since forgotten how to blush. And the mention of sex aroused him instantly. "I assure you that I'm a decent fellow," he said sheepishly, worried that she would feel the change in his body. "I'm William..."

"Oh no! Not another William!"

"I won't tell you how much my kitchen is worth."

"Eavesdropper."

He smiled and continued, "I'm William Darcy," then waited to see her response.

"Elizabeth Bennet," she replied. *Good, she doesn't seem to recognise my name.*

She tried again to free herself, but the thread was still tightly wrapped around his shirt button, and so she abandoned the effort.

He breathed out a sigh of relief. At least they could pretend he didn't have a hard on.

They chatted absently during the ten-minute walk to Darcy's townhouse, and he found that he liked her sense of humour. But the townhouse, when they arrived, was pitch black. *How strange,* he thought as he opened the door. *Where are Mrs Reynolds and Georgiana?*

"Surprise! Surprise!"

Darcy frowned, startled and displeased. *What is Caroline Bingley doing here?*

"Happy Birthday!"

The lights came on, revealing a crowd made up of Georgiana, his uncle's family and Bingley's family. There were balloons, decoration and music. A camera flashed, before the people in the house became aware that Darcy was not alone.

Caroline, wearing a tight orange leopard-print bodysuit and a large orange headband, tried to jump forward to grab Darcy's arm, but her brother held her back.

"Hey, Darce, it seems you planned a more private celebration. You two started undressing on the street already?" Richard was, in fact, winking broadly at Darcy's lower body. He gave Richard an angry stare, silently forbidding his cousin to mention his arousal. And, while Darcy might have forgotten his own birthday, he wasn't going to let go of this special woman, especially if the alternative was to be fawned all over by Caroline for the whole evening.

He wrapped his arm more tightly around Elizabeth and said, "I'm sure you won't mind starting the party without Elizabeth and me ..."

"...Since we'll be busy upstairs for the whole night," Elizabeth said, and winked back at Richard as the rest of the guests gaped at them.

*I will hold her to this, and have her spend the night here,* Darcy vowed to himself. Together, they walked up the stairs at a rapid pace, with the squeaking scream from Caroline ringing in their ears.

Well, did they appear again for Darcy's birthday party, that night? The author leaves that for you to speculate.

Darcy and Elizabeth tied the knot six months later, after he received almost all 9s from her on every aspect of her rating. And Richard sent them an enlarged photo of their infamous grand entrance to that fateful birthday party as a wedding present.

*What if Elizabeth came to Pemberley to apologize?*

## Speedy Speedo Valentine

"Let's shake on it!" Richard said with a smirk, and squeezed his cousin's hand.

Georgiana gave him a scowl and returned his handshake, then returned to her side of the net with a determined pace.

"What did you promise that devil?" Darcy asked his sister absently when she arrived at his side. He hadn't gotten a good sleep, last night. In fact, his sleep had frequently been troubled in the past two months, since his return from Kent. Every night, Elizabeth Bennet invaded his dreams, telling him that he was arrogant and selfish, and that she wouldn't shag him if he was the last man in the world.

He hadn't wanted to come along on this picnic, let alone play a game of volleyball with Richard, Caroline and Georgiana.

"I agreed that the losing team will have to wear swimming costumes in the office for the Valentine week promotion." Georgiana said.

"What?"

"Well, Richard has a big mouth! He laughed at my new hat. You've never lost to him before, and I'm sure we'll win, so..." Georgiana subsided into a pout.

Darcy shook his head and took his position. Thankful, at least, that Caroline wasn't on his team. He put his mind on the game. Unfortunately, he only had half of his mind in Derbyshire, the other half being with Elizabeth, so his team was promptly crushed by Richard alone.

On the Monday morning of Valentine Week, with a cheery grin, Richard Fitzwilliam intercepted his cousin as he arrived for work at Pemberley Winery.

"Hey, where's your Speedo?" Richard raised his eyebrow and leaned on the door frame.

Darcy frowned and tried to push past him. "I promised you nothing."

Richard dug out a pair of swimming trunks from the shopping bag he was carrying and waved them in front of Darcy.

The latter tried to brush past, but Richard pinned him against the wall.

"Georgie promised *for* you. Since the day you pushed a frog down my pants when I was fifteen, I've been waiting for this day. I'm not letting you off so easily. Everyone in the office knows about the bet. If you don't want to change, I can help you." He bared his teeth in an evil grin as he reached for Darcy's tie.

"Get your hands off me!" Darcy growled.

"You only grace the business office anyway. What are you afraid of? Georgie is the one who has to conduct tours."

"She's wearing a bikini to greet guests?" Darcy grabbed Richard's tie this time. "How could you let her do that?"

"You don't have to worry. The marketing girls in the office want to support her, so they're all going to wear swimsuits, this week. And it's a one-piece, not bikini. They even came up with a marketing idea: Sizzling Valentine Week. You know, beach music, fake sand and imitation palm trees. A free BBQ for guests."

Darcy tried to wrestle his temper back into its box. "Okay, okay, give me the swim trunks," he said, and took the Speedo into the men's room.

When he came out of the cubicle, Richard was waiting for him. "No shirt, Mr. Darcy," he said sweetly.

Reluctantly, Darcy took off the shirt and began to gather his clothes, but Richard snatched them up and shoved them into the shopping bag.

"I'll get them back to you at the end of the day," Richard said, and headed for the men's room door. "Have a great day, Mr. Hairy."

Darcy chased after him, pretending to raise his fist. Richard's laughter echoed as he turned back to make a face at Darcy before running away at top speed from his menacing cousin.

As Darcy reached the turn-off to his section, he walked on quickly, increasingly self-conscious as every employee turned to stare at him.

"Good morning, Mr. Darcy." Mr. Reynolds chuckled at he looked at his big boss wearing nothing but a pair of swim trunks. "It's a hot day."

"A day when business mixes with pleasure." Mrs. Reynolds giggled at she scanned at her boss in his black Speedo, white socks and dark Bally shoes.

Darcy nodded and increased his pace yet again.

When he finally reached his office, he let out a sigh of relief. In two steps, he reached the cabinet where he kept a fresh change of clothes, and pulled it open.

It was empty! Damn! Richard was very thorough.

Admitting defeat, Darcy sat down behind his desk and started working. But his day was constantly disturbed by every employee, male or female, who could think of an excuse to come into his office.

By one o'clock, he'd had enough. He rang Mrs. Reynolds to ask to have some lunch brought in, but she was not answering. In fact, every secretary in her section seemed to have disappeared, as well.

"Where the hell is everybody?" Darcy swore. He was hungry and cranky. And he wasn't about to risk calling for take-away. There was no telling what the pizza delivery lad would say when he saw Darcy in Speedo in the office.

He waited for another half an hour, but there was still no trace of Mrs. Reynolds. Deciding to raid the staff kitchen, Darcy tried to plan the least 'exposed' route to his destination.

The back garden!

Yes, that would be a longer route, but he would not have to walk past any desks or offices along the way.

So decided, he stalked along the deserted back corridor, through the fire exit and out to the back garden, where a blast of cold air greeted him. However, as he made the turn that would take him to the staff kitchen, he was shocked to see Elizabeth Bennet there, sitting on a bench beneath the old chestnut tree.

He stopped dead in his stride, while she jumped up from the bench. She was wearing a green sundress with lovely floral pattern, looking like a siren straight from his dreams.

"William!"

"Elizabeth!"

Her eyes widened as her gaze travelled from his hairy torso down to his tight Speedo, his muscular thighs and, incongruously, his shiny shoes.

He swallowed and tried to explain. “It’s Sizzling Valentine Week at Pemberley Winery. We all dressed in swimming costumes, but I forgot to bring my thongs.”

Her lips curved upward into a smile, and she said in a husky voice, “Yes, it is steamy hot here.”

Darcy’s heartbeat quickened. *She smiles very seductively. And her eyes are focused on my chest, or even lower. Has she accepted my explanation about Jane and Charles and Wickham?* He decided to test the water.

In two strides, he stood mere inches from her. Taking her hands in his, he gave her a cheerful kiss on her cheek, then stepped back slightly. “Welcome to Pemberley Winery! Are you here on tour?”

She shook her head and licked her lips. Drawing in a deep breath, she looked him squarely in the eyes. “Actually, I came to thank you for sending Charles back to Jane.”

Locking his eyes on hers, and squeezing her hands gently, he murmured, “There’s no need to thank me. I’m just righting a wrong.”

Elizabeth sighed. “It wasn’t your fault. They’re both adults. I shouldn’t blame you for Charles’s own indecision.” She leaned closer to him. “And I’m sorry for ever believing that sleazy Wickham.”

“It’s great that you’re here.” Darcy breathed the words slowly and lowered his mouth to touch her moist lips, allowing her time to evade him, if she wanted.

But instead of snubbing him as she had done in Kent, Elizabeth returned his kiss. It had taken her two months to gather her courage and admit to herself that Darcy was a nice guy, a good guy, a great, hunky guy who loved her, but she had finally faced facts. Upon doing so, she had made up her mind to come all the way to Derbyshire on the pretence of thanking him...but really to see if he still wanted her, because, now, she felt drawn to him, wanted him...maybe even loved him. She opened her mouth and sucked his upper lip with zest, willing to risk showing him her desire.

She felt his tongue travel over her teeth seductively. The gesture sent a shiver down her spine. Then the tables turned as he began to suck her lips and thrust his tongue into her mouth, probing her flesh, making her wet with passion.

His hot hands moved over her butt, squeezing it hard as he pressed her body to his. Feeling an answering frenzy, she wrapped her hands around his back, kneading the hard muscles there. When her hands found their way inside his swim trunks and grasped his pert bottom, he released her mouth and groaned aloud, like a wolf howling to his mate.

The world seemed to stop in that instant.

They gazed at each other, caught up in the throes of yearning. Their eyes met in silent communion. Then, taking her hand, Darcy led her back toward his office.

Once they were inside, with the door shut and locked, Darcy pressed her against it and meshed his mouth with hers, his tongue continuing the thrusting motions he had first initiated outside in the back garden. As he sucked her tongue demandingly, his body rubbed against her, transferring heat and sweat to her skin through her thin dress. His arousal sizzled against her, making her body swelter.

His hands slid up her thighs to her panties and tore them off. In response, Elizabeth latched onto the elastic band of his Speedo and pulled it down.

Not waiting for her to finish her job, Darcy thrust into her wet entrance while the Speedo was still half way down his thighs.

At that, her hands lost their hold on the fabric, shifting to clutch his buttocks instead. As his thick, pulsing cock stretched her tight muscles, her nails dug into his flesh.

Inch by inch, his shaft spread her sex wider, while his hands pulled down the straps of the sundress, freeing the fabric to pool at her waist. Unclasping her bra and tossing it aside, he stroked her breasts fiercely.

Elizabeth's heart raced, and her breathing grew quick and shallow. Leaning against the door for support, she felt extreme pleasure from three different fronts. His tongue was thrusting into her mouth, stirring up a volcanic storm in her head. His thumbs and fingers were rubbing her nipples, puckering them to hard pebbles. And his powerful cock was invading her core, his body pumping in and out of her with vigour. As his hard rod stroked her inner muscles, he ignited a sizzling sensation all through her body, from her sex, up her breasts to unite with the storm in her brain.

On fire, she peaked in a scant handful of minutes.

Trembling, squeezing him hard with her hands and her sex, she tipped him over the edge, as well. His blazing shaft throbbed inside her, vibrating as his essence fountained into her.

When Darcy finally withdrew his tongue from her mouth, his hands from her nipples, and himself from her core, Elizabeth felt the loss keenly. Savouring their connection, she slid her hands up and wrapped them around his neck, then folded her legs around his waist. Resting her head on his shoulder, she kissed his earlobe.

He embraced her, with his arms positioned around her bottom, walking awkwardly since his Speedo was still at mid-thigh. Sensing his predicament, she giggled. He grinned back and continued on. After a few bumps and turns, he finally brought her to where they could lie down on the couch. Snuggling down besides her, he brushed a few strands of wet hair from her brow and kissed her forehead.

"You're sizzling hot," she said, suppressing a laugh.

"You're the fiery one." He nipped her nose.

She trailed her fingertips over his lips.

His eyes grew dark, and he licked her fingers. Within seconds, he was sucking them wet, savouring every inch of her small, delicate fingers.

Her eyes widened. *How can he arouse me so fast?* She felt the dampness on her fingers, transmitting a path of lightning along her nerve endings from her arm to her breasts and down to the apex of her thighs.

She squirmed, and her legs touched his. Immediately, she sensed the rise of his shaft.

"So soon?" she asked in wonder.

He licked her fingers one last time before replying, "Only for you."

"Flatterer!" She shivered.

Grinning, he moved her on top of him. Understanding his desire, she braced her hands on his hard chest and shifted her hips so that her wet folds rubbed his rod.

"Ah!"

They gasped in mutual pleasure. Then his hands moved to fondle her breasts, shaping them to firm peaks, before he raised his head to lave her nipples, one after the other.

She panted, head thrown back, and squeezed her legs around his hips involuntarily.

"Urghhhhhh!" He groaned out loud again before urging her to take control.

Raising her hips, she positioned herself above his raging arousal. Their gazes locked in a passionate connection as she lowered herself onto him. His proud rod thrust into her to the hilt, torching her muscles to red-hot sensitivity.

After enjoying the fullness of his manhood for a few seconds, she was urged back into action by his hands.

They clasped her bouncy breasts again, rubbing and twisting her twin peaks.

The bliss of her upper body made her move her lower body in a frenzy. She rode him hard and fast, racing toward her destination at break-neck speed. Soon, she cried out in another massive orgasm, then crumpled to rest limply atop his body.

Lifting her free of him, he turned her over onto all fours on the sofa, then plunged into her again, drawing her hips towards him. Thrusting into her forcefully from behind, he savoured every movement, groaning loudly.

As his hips smacked against her bottom, the slapping sound kept time with his groans. A few minutes later, Elizabeth's post-orgasmic haze sharpened into fresh arousal, and she soon experienced yet another mind-blowing climax.

This time, he peaked with her. They pulsed and trembled for long minutes before finally flopping down onto the couch with a thump.

Silence reigned. They drifted into a satisfied doze, until a knock on the door brought them back to reality.

"Yes?" Darcy called out.

"William, I bring you lunch." The high pitch voice of Caroline Bingley sent shivers through both Darcy and Elizabeth.

"I just had...the best lunch. You don't have to bother." His hands smoothed along the creamy curves on Elizabeth's body, and he bit her breast tenderly.

Elizabeth nearly giggled but managed to cover her mouth with her hand.

Caroline kept knocking on the door, trying to persuade Darcy to open it for her. But he didn't reply her. He was too busy exploring every inch of Elizabeth's body leisurely with his mouth, until after half an hour, a defeated Caroline Bingley finally left them.

"I love you, my hot Lizzy." Darcy proclaimed.

In that moment, Elizabeth realised for certain that she loved him, too. Otherwise, she would never have made love to him in such an abandoned manner. "I love you too, sizzling Darcy."

When Richard returned to Darcy's office at the end of the day, he found it empty except for a scrap of Speedo and a bra!

How did Darcy and Elizabeth leave unnoticed? She went to his car to retrieve a fresh set of clothes for him, as she didn't want anyone to ogle her Mr. Darcy again. Then the two of them left in her car, which she had parked near the back garden. She had gotten lost on her way to Pemberley Winery and had accidentally – fortunately for them both – entered it through the back.

Where had Mrs. Reynolds and the secretary pools gone? The beach-themed cellar door had attracted so many unexpected visitors that they were requested by the Marketing Department to help out.

And what about Richard's revenge? Darcy was "not reachable" by him for five days. Darcy whisked Elizabeth to a real beach in the Maldives for the remaining of that sizzling Valentine Week. On Valentine's Day, he proposed marriage again, and was warmly accepted.

*What if Santa gave Mr. Darcy a special gift?*

## Chimney Damper

Caroline Bingley tugged the neckline of the scarlet Santa dress lower and puffed her breasts higher. Then she turned to look at the hemline, to make sure that it only barely covered her sexy butt.

"Perfect!" she murmured. It was Christmas Eve and she had a very important mission to fulfil.

She walked out of her room and down the corridor, to the rear of the house. When she reached the spiral staircase, she climbed it carefully. She had asked a maid to make sure that her route would be clear and easily recognisable in the dark. She did not intend to dirty her nails or muss her hair along the way. So far, the maid seemed to have done a satisfactory job.

Finally, she reached the roof of Netherfield. The moon was bright, and she had no trouble finding the chimney that led to Mr. Darcy's room. After all, she had been planning this Christmas surprise for some time.

After her brother Charles had defied her wishes and leased this backwater country estate, she had racked her brain for a way to turn the situation around. She had commissioned a thorough survey of Netherfield's design and, after studying it, had decided that it would be the perfect place to seduce her heart's desire.

First, she persuaded her brother to invite his friend to spend the holiday season with them in this 'unexplored' realm. Then she had arranged for Mr. Darcy to be given a spacious room that had an electric fireplace and a separate, unused chimney. She had even undergone a breast augmentation procedure especially for the occasion.

Her plan was to parachute into the billionaire's room in her sexy Santa dress. With the amount of alcohol that he and her brother had consumed during the Christmas feast, he should be quite susceptible to her seductive advances, ready to have his Christmas fantasy come true. However...

"Umph..."

The chimney, to her consternation, looked rather small. As instructed, the maid had secured one end of a rope ladder to the side of the chimney. Caroline pulled to make sure that it was knotted tightly before lowering the ladder into the shaft.

Reaching in, she ran her fingertip along the edge of the chimney. "Great, it's clean!"

Reassured, she began her climb down the ladder, moving carefully. One...two...three... four... So far, her plan seemed to be working well.

But, two-thirds of the way down the chimney, disaster struck as it became apparent that the maid hadn't cleaned it all the way down. Caroline's hands and body came in contact with soot that had been there for over a hundred years.

Brimming with anger, she kicked the side of the shaft with fury – and slipped. Luckily, the chimney narrowed at that juncture, prevented her fall. But perhaps she was not all *that* lucky because, as she contorted herself and regained her footing on the ladder and tried to continue her descent, she found that she could not move an inch. Her new breasts were stuck in the narrow neck of the chimney.

After a few wiggles, she could feel something strange within her breasts. Hastily, she stopped moving, afraid that her new body parts might burst.

As panic rose within her, she abandoned stealth and screamed aloud, hoping that Mr. Darcy would hear her and come to her rescue. Finally, after several minutes of crying out at the top of her voice, she heard voices rising up the chimney shaft from below. Holding her breath, she listened intently...and heard a woman's voice.

"You are the most arrogant jerk I've ever met!"

That was Miss Eliza Bennet, the country bumpkin who had shown up to visit her sick sister, without invitation, and had had the audacity to accept Charles's invitation to stay. What was she doing in Mr. Darcy's bedroom?

"Jerk or not, I have the hots for you!" His tipsy voice was uncharacteristically filled with emotion. *How could my Mr. Darcy possibly have such a poor taste,* Caroline thought?

Then came the sound of a slap, and some shoving of furniture was audible. It then grew quiet. Caroline prepared to shout for help again...then hesitated when she heard a moaning sound.

Perhaps her Mr. Darcy had been injured by that uncouth Miss Eliza. Caroline debated what to do for a few minutes, then tried banging on the wall of the chimney shaft.

The sound was then echoed by a series of rhythmic smacking sounds from below, followed by Eliza's shrill voice exclaiming, "Yes! Harder! Faster!"

What on earth was happening below? Caroline's mind raced... and reached an altogether unacceptable conclusion. Squealing In fury, she shrieked, "I'm stuck! Help me! Mr. Darcy, help me!"

The room below grew abruptly silent for a moment. Then the slamming noise below began again, more urgently than before.

Outraged, Caroline pushed against the confining walls with a strength born of rage.

Suddenly, part of the wall inside the chimney crumbled and gave way, and she felt her body dropping down. Reaching out blindly, she tried to brace herself to break her fall. Instead, she landed on the floor with a jolting thump. Luckily she rolled and landed on the soft thick carpet.

As she brushed away the choking soot from the old chimney, she saw that her Mr. Darcy was seated on the floor, with Miss Eliza straddling him, both breathing even more heavily than Caroline.

To her horror, she saw that her heart's desire had his trousers down to his ankles. The slut's skirts covered his hips, and he had his face buried in her breasts. Eliza's blouse was open all the way down to her waist. Her hands were tangled in his hair, while his were apparently gripping her ass, judging by where they vanished beneath her skirts.

"Let go of my Mr. Darcy!" Caroline roared.

They both turned to look at her with wide eyes.

"Why are you wearing a smutty Santa dress and coming down the chimney into Darcy's room?" Elizabeth demanded.

"I'm his Christmas present. As if that's any of your business!" Caroline stood up and tried to pull the insolent invader off her man.

But Elizabeth ignored her, turning back to look at Darcy and exclaim aloud, "You're all hard and hot again!"

He grinned, then scowled at Caroline, "Leave my room at once, fake Santa! I'm in the middle of a bout of mind-blowing sex. This is the best Christmas I've ever had."

Choking on soot and indignation, Caroline scrambled for the door. Behind her, she heard Eliza ask, "But why is her bosom so uneven?"

"Don't know. Don't care. I'm too busy worshiping your gorgeous, pert breasts, my dearest loveliest Elizabeth!" Darcy's slurred voice pierced Caroline's ears.

Escaping into the hallway, Caroline slammed the door shut behind herself and stormed off down the hallway... only to stop in her tracks as she caught sight of herself in the hall mirror. The hateful chit's words had been all too true, for Caroline's reflection revealed that her struggle inside the chimney had burst her right implant, leaving her with a decidedly lopsided look with which to greet the new year.

*What if Lizzy was an inventor?*

## The Fly Rips the Fly

Seated on the lawn of Oxford University, Jane tried one last time to change her sister's mind. "You're sure you don't want to come?"

"Your history professor trashed us. Why would I want to go and listen to his antiquated lecture? I have better thing to do here," Elizabeth said firmly as she worked to fix the lips of the robofly.

"But Mr. Darcy is so handsome! Six foot three, broad shoulders, darkest eyes, long eyelashes, and all that lush, dark, wavy hair... If Charles wasn't my soul mate, and Darcy wasn't his best friend, I would be acting like all of the other girls in class, wearing their see-through tops, push-up bras and mini-skirts." Jane sighed. "And he was not belittling scientists. He simply said that they should learn about the past in order to create a better future. In fact, I think he has the hots for you."

"Ha ha. Are you trying to be funny? And I don't think that learning about how we had war after war will help us to prevent another war. Damn! Caroline's mouth is deformed." Elizabeth threw down the electric drill in frustration.

"Oh Lizzy, you shouldn't call your robofly Caroline! What if she heard you?"

"So what if she did? Your soul mate's sister is an annoying specimen. She fawns over rich men like a pesky fly. See? I even made the eyes with small circles in different shades of orange, exactly the way that Caroline looks when she wears her designer sunglasses. I think I'll win the Inventor Competition *and* the £50,000. It will help Mary to pay her grad school fee."

"All right then, I'll leave you with your invention. I'm meeting Charles first, before I go to the lecture. You can still join me, if you change your mind. It starts in about an hour's time. See you!" Jane gave Elizabeth a kiss on the cheek and left.

Elizabeth was happy to see her sister go. She was determined to make Caroline the Robofly's lips perfect, and Jane had been distracting her with her talk of old-fashioned Mr. Darcy.

The robofly was about the size of the palm of her hand, and Elizabeth had packed a lot of functionality into her small invention. Caroline could fly, grab things with her six legs, and hum as she zipped through the air. But the hairy mouth just didn't seem right.

Half an hour later, Caroline the Robofly was ready for her next test flight. Elizabeth turned the remote control to 'On' and launched the fly.

"Yes!" Elizabeth exclaimed, and put up one hand in triumph. Caroline's wings were quite steady, and the humming sound was perfect. After a few minutes of circling, however, Caroline the Robofly suddenly lost altitude and crash-landed on a man passing by.

"Oh, sorry!" Elizabeth rushed to the man's side...and her eyes widened as she saw that Caroline's crooked lips had latched onto the fly of the man's trousers. "Oh, I *am* sorry!" she reiterated, and raised her eyes to meet those of the stranger.

But he was no stranger. He was Mr. Darcy, the history professor, and he was scowling at her.

"What is...that?" he demanded, and pointed at the palm-sized fly on his fly.

"That's Caroline," Elizabeth blurted.

"Caroline...as in Charles's sister?" His countenance darkened.

"No, it's just my invention. A robotic fly that I named Caroline. Her mouth is deformed. I mean...it has a design problem."

"I can see that." He grabbed Caroline's body and tried to pull her off, but her mouth grasped the material tightly. "Remove her, please. I have a lecture in half an hour."

"No, don't harm it! Let me try." Elizabeth tried to pull the robofly off but Caroline wouldn't budge. Moreover, the shaking motions on his trousers seemed to be making Mr. Darcy hot and flustered. Elizabeth hesitated, afraid to persist but equally afraid to give up.

Darcy had known Elizabeth for six months, through his friend Charles Bingley. After their initial clash about historic and scientific importance, he realised that he found her both smart and pretty. In fact, he had been itching to ask her out for quite a while. Now, with her tugging at the area closest to his manhood, he feared that he would disgrace himself in front of her, on the public lawn in the university. But what else could he do? The time for his lecture was fast approaching, and Caroline had to go!

As Elizabeth became aware of the growing bulge under his trousers, she raised her eyes and gave him a darting glance, then swallowed hard and turned her attention to the remote control instead. Using an electric drill, she opened the control box, moved several bits of wiring around, and started Caroline up again.

With a screeching sound, Caroline the Robofly finally released Darcy's trousers...but the corner of her mouth was still snagged on the fabric of his trousers. As she flew up awkwardly, she ripped Darcy's trousers open, right where his bulge was.

"Oh!" Elizabeth exclaimed, aghast.

He tried to untangle the fabric, grabbing for Caroline's head to prevent her from flying off and taking the entire front of his trousers with her. But it was not until she had ripped off the majority of the fly – and part of his underpants – that she subsided and tumbled to the ground.

"You killed Caroline!" Elizabeth cried.

"She split my pants!" responded Darcy, his hands now cupped to cover his private parts.

Looking at him, Elizabeth suddenly forgot about the demise of her invention and began to grin, then giggle, then laugh out loud.

Her laughter was infectious. A grin curved Darcy's mouth, and he found the courage to say, "I'll ring the office and ask them to have my assistant take care of my lecture. You invented Caroline the Monster, and so you are morally responsible for her actions. I expect you to compensate me, hugely." He quirked one eyebrow. "At your place!"

Her gaze travelled from his dimpled smile to his sparkling eyes, then down to the impressive bulge he was attempting to cover. Licking her lips, she decided that she agreed with Jane: Mr. Darcy, professor of ancient history, was indeed quite yummy...and it appeared that he did have the hots for her.

She took off her jacket, revealing the halter top she wore beneath it, and was happy to hear him gasp. "Tie this around your waist," she suggested, holding out the jacket to him.

And they held hands as they ran back to her apartment.

The next morning, Darcy was awakened by the shrill sound of Caroline the Robofly as it dive-bombed toward him. His hands instinctively moved down to protect his naked cock.

Elizabeth, who sat nude at the end of the bed, holding the remote control, burst out laughing. "Caroline won't bite your impressive asset any more. I've removed her mouth."

"Naughty little inventor!" He scolded, and pulled her down on top of him so that he could proceed to kiss and bite every inch of her body in loving retaliation.

*What if Mr. Darcy kidnapped Elizabeth?*

## Mistaken Identity

"Let go of me!" Elizabeth shrieked, but she was pushed into a limo which then sped away at high speed. She tried to wrench the door open, but it was locked. How could this be happening on the streets of Meryton? It was a quiet, picturesque, country town, and she had lived there all her life until her moved to Cambridge, a month earlier.

Inside the speeding car, on the plush leather seat opposite, a man in a tuxedo sat with his arms folded across his chest, staring at her. He had dark, curly hair, broad shoulders and a cold expression. *At least he doesn't look like an axe murderer*, she thought. *Then again, there's no telling, these days. He could be a serial killer, for all I know.*

"Who are you?" she demanded. "Why are you kidnapping me?"

"Where is Richard?" he asked in return.

"Richard?" She frowned, thinking hard about all of her friends. "I don't know any Richard. You've got the wrong person. Let me go or I'll call the police."

"I don't think so, Miss Bennet. Kidnapping is a serious crime. And you're the one who's keeping Richard. It's late and I'm tired. Tell me where he is and I may put in some good words for you with the police."

*How did he know my name?* Elizabeth wondered wildly. "No, I don't know who this Richard is and no, I haven't kidnapped him. I'm just a librarian working at the university. You've got the wrong person."

"Librarian? That's not what Richard says you are," he sneered. "You either tell me where Richard is, right now, or you'll stay with me until you do."

"How many times do I have to tell you that I don't know him!"

"Don't take me for a fool. I've seen the memory stick. You know him – shockingly well, in fact."

"What memory stick?"

"The one with scores of photos of you opening your legs and letting Richard suck your pussy to heaven."

Elizabeth's face turned bright red. Anger rose in her chest, and she flew across the limo.

*Snap!*

She slapped him across the face.

Her hand landed against his angular cheek, loud and clear. She gasped, not believing what she had done. She had never hit another person in her life.

As her body froze, Darcy grabbed her hand and pulled her against him.

"Wildcat!" He said, and his eyes flashed with fury. Her fierce struggles rubbed her body against his repeatedly, causing the blood to rush from his head. Her breasts were pert and lush. Her nipples had peaked as she battled against him. When he succeeded in pinning her hands behind her back, he could feel her narrow waist and rounded, bouncy bottom. What a wild woman!

He hadn't studied the photos that came with the ransom note for very long. He was not a pervert, and he found the lush body of this gold digger disgusting. His cousin, Richard, who had met her at a night club frequented by footballers, had told Darcy that she was a good, easy fuck once he plied her with enough wine and gifts. The two had been seeing each other for the past month.

Given all of that, Darcy didn't know why, in close proximity, this slut seemed to have the power to bewitch him. Her eyes seemed to convey a myriad of emotions: innocence, fire and strength. But those feelings could not be true of someone who spent her young life trying to feed off of rich men. Still, her overused body was creating havoc in his, causing his cock to rise.

"Stop struggling." His face was inches away from hers. "If you're in such a desperate need of a million pounds, you can open your legs for me a few times. After all, the Darcy name is worth more than its weight in gold. There's no need to involve Richard." Against his better judgment, he made her an offer and rubbed his arousal against her thigh, making his interest clear to her.

The mere touch nearly undid him. He drew in a deep breath to calm his rioting blood, but that resulted in him inhaling her lavender scent. It was unexpected and refreshing, far different from most manufactured perfumes.

"You're sick!" Elizabeth spat. "I've never slept with this Richard, and I'll never sleep with you. Let me go!"

"Your voice is hurting my ears," he said, and silenced her by lowering his lips to capture hers in a kiss.

But she wouldn't give in to such an assault, and bit him hard on the lip.

He yelped in pain, and she took the opportunity to scramble free of him and retreat to the opposite side of the seat. "Don't try that again," she threatened menacingly, brandishing the fountain pen she had grabbed from his breast pocket, "or I won't be responsible for my actions."

He brushed the blood from his lip and glared at her.

"Now tell your men to stop the car."

"Why should I? My bodyguards can disarm you easily." He folded his arms across his chest again.

Elizabeth glared at him, drawing in deep breaths. "Then let us start again, right at the beginning, Mr. Darcy." She paused for a moment, gathering her wits, determined to get right to the heart of the matter. Now that she had a small weapon in her hand and had retreated as far away from him as the luxurious car would allow, she felt a little more in control. "You were sent a memory stick, containing photos that were supposedly of me...er...having sex with this 'Richard.' I assume that he is a friend of yours and has disappeared, and that you believe, from the note that came with the memory stick, that his release depends upon you providing someone with a million pounds. And you claim that this 'Richard' has told you that he knows me? And that I am not a librarian working at the University of Cambridge?" She shook her head in consternation. "Who is this 'Richard' to you?"

"If you want to continue to play this game, I can indulge you," Darcy replied with a sneer. "Richard is my cousin. And he told me that he met you at a night club in London a month ago, Miss Lydia Bennet."

"Lydia?" Elizabeth exclaimed in surprise. "But she's my youngest sister."

"I saw the photos. It's you who was moaning in ecstasy with Richard, whatever your name may be."

"You have my bag," she pointed out archly. "Look at my driver's license. I'm Elizabeth Bennet, not Lydia."

Darcy wanted to salute her acting skill. Had she anticipated that he would resist paying the ransom? Did she, in fact, plan to land a bigger fish, like himself? Well, she had fared excellently, so far, for he was hooked. He didn't even mind that she had slept with Richard. As long as she was willing to warm his bed until he'd gotten his fill of her delectable body, he would be willing to reward her handsomely.

A voice in his mind told him that he was crazy. He had never had to pay for sex. True, some of the models and starlets he'd dated in his younger years had been after his money and fame, but he had outgrown that phase. He was more selective in his choice of women now. Perhaps that was the problem. He hadn't gotten laid for several months, and the spirited resistance of this woman sparked his interest. Not just that. His whole body seemed to be on fire from that not-so-fortunate kiss that had lasted for a few brief seconds. Her lips were lush, and her mouth had tasted of bittersweet chocolate. The blaze in her eyes promised a heavenly response when he finally got her voluptuous body under his hard muscles. He intended to fuck her to oblivion and make her forget all the other men she had ever had.

Giving her a sceptical look, he picked up her bag. Not a designer one, he noted. Raising his eyebrow, he opened the bag and started searching.

A book? Did she have to be so obvious, to pretend to be a librarian? *The Importance of Being Earnest*? Perhaps she was learning about how to manage her multiple identities from Earnest.

A minimum of cosmetics. Hmm. That didn't fit her profile. Darcy frowned and glanced at this so-called 'Elizabeth' for a second. She didn't have a lot of makeup on her face, just now. Just a lip gloss that highlighted her sultry lips. But perhaps she saved that for her wild nights.

The wallet was made of simple dark-blue leather without any brand markings. Strange. He flipped it open. Yes, there was the license. Elizabeth Bennet, aged 23, auburn hair, brown eyes, 159 cm (5 foot 2) in height.

Wait! The woman in the ransom photos hadn't been that short...

"How tall is your sister?" Darcy asked, almost sighing with relief as he asked. This young woman was *not* the whore who had slept with Richard.

"Lydia? About 179 (5 foot 8)." The tension in Elizabeth's face seemed to ease. "Now can you believe me when I tell you that I have nothing to do with your cousin's disappearance?"

He pondered for a minute. "Not so fast. You might be the mastermind!"

"Your wealth doesn't seem to have improved your mind," she retorted. "Why would I send you photos of myself to help you find me, if I was really the kidnapper?"

"My mind is perfectly sound. You could have faked the driver's license."

"Show me the photos then, and I can tell you how they were Photoshopped."

He shook his head obstinately. "No matter whether you're involved or not, Miss Elizabeth – if that's really your name – it's better for me to have you here," Darcy said slowly, his eyes scanning her body, "with me, until this is resolved."

"You can't kidnap me in order to find your kidnapped cousin!" she exclaimed. Her face turned bright red, and her chest heaved up and down in indignation. Watching her, Darcy almost forgot about the problem of Richard. He wanted to be the one to make her scream and her body pulse. But the car stopped, at just that moment.

He bent forward, fast as a panther, disarmed her, got out of the car, pulled her out and slung her over his shoulder, in a single flurry of movement.

Elizabeth's heart skipped. How could he not believe her? What had Lydia done, this time? She could feel the angry Mr. Darcy's hands on her bottom and upper thighs, restricting her kicks. She tried to scratch his back, but he was wearing a thick tuxedo. There were two men standing by the limo but they didn't come to her aid, no matter how much she yelled. She could see that they were inside a garage, then an elevator. It seemed to be a private building, for they didn't encounter anyone as Mr. Darcy strode past a spacious sitting room and into a masculine bedroom, where he tossed her onto the bed.

Before Elizabeth could get her bearings and make a run for the door, he threw a packet of photographs toward her. She stopped dead as she caught a glimpse of the images. Every one of them was scandalous...and the face was, in fact, hers! But the body, in a variety of pornographic poses as it pleasured this 'Richard,' was definitely *not* hers.

She drew a deep breath. "Apparently you've figured out that this woman is taller than I am."

Darcy, standing between her and the door, nodded. "Is that your sister Lydia?"

With a heavy sigh, she nodded and pointed at one of the photos. "She has a diamond tattoo on her right butt cheek..."

"Which you don't have?" He raised his brows and added, with a curl of his lip, "Then I'm sure you'll understand when I ask you to take off your skirt and let me have a look."

Her eyes flashed with dangerous light. "Give me my phone. I'll track down Lydia for you."

"Just like that?"

Clearly, he still didn't believe her. "I told you already, Mr. Darcy," she said, rolling her eyes with exasperation, "Lydia wouldn't send you photos that could identify her – or me – so easily. The person who sent you this ransom note is a dimwit."

He nodded toward the phone by the head of the bed. "Use that speaker phone. It will record the conversation, and I'll be able to hear both of you."

Fuming, Elizabeth tried to reach her eldest sister, Jane, then several of Lydia's friends, before she finally tracked down her youngest sister. "Where the hell are you?" Elizabeth yelled at the phone, as there was loud music blasting from the end of the other line.

"How about 'I miss you, my dear Lydia' before you start shouting at me?"

"I've no time for chitchat, Lydia! There's a mad man named Darcy here who thinks I've kidnapped your boyfriend, Richard."

Lydia burst out laughing. "Rich, do you know a dickhead called Darcy? He thinks you've been kidnapped by Lizzy. How droll!" Her piercing laughter was echoed by several women. But the happy cheers were interrupted by a man's loud scream of pain. "Darcy, help!"

"That's Richard!" Darcy dashed to sit near Elizabeth and lowered his head to speak to the phone. "Have you been harmed? Is this Lydia hurting you? I'll send my bodyguards and call in the police. Where are you?"

"Knebworth House..." Another man replied, but his revelation was cut short by Lydia's voice.

"Poosh, you stop right there, Dickhead Darcy. Rich is enjoying this. Isn't he?" Lydia asked someone.

"Definitely!" one woman replied.

"Immensely!" another agreed.

"He asked for it."

"How come...?" Elizabeth's murmur was drowned out by another loud screeching sound from Richard. Then he shouted, "No!"

"Who's with you, Richard?" Darcy called out anxiously, his face knotted with concern.

"Darcy, call off your body guards! The ransom note was just a joke." Richard said.

Another man howled in pain. "I'm dying! Rescue us! These women are crazy..." The wail of anguish grew sharper. "...They tie us up...!"

"Wickham!" Darcy and Elizabeth exclaimed in unison.

"Yes, Wicky is with us, too," Lydia said, and dissolved into giggles with the other women.

Elizabeth gasped. "Lydia, is that Aunt Phillips and Mary with you?" She glared at Darcy and fired another question at Lydia. "What are you doing to those men? Release them immediately! Mr. Darcy said he wouldn't let me go until Richard is safe."

"Why don't you bring your Mr. Darcy here, Lizzy?" a woman with a serious voice asked. "He'll love it. We're having a heavy metal party at Knebworth House, and you're both invited."

"Mary, what are you up to?" Elizabeth demanded. "What kind of party is that? Richard and Wickham sound like they're in agony!"

"It's a Brazilian waxing party," the voice of an older woman said. "Mr. Darcy, I'm Lizzy's aunt, Mrs. Phillips. Don't worry about your friends. They agreed to the party, and they will look marvellous after we wax them completely. I've done their chests and the hair on their toes already. Next we'll be working on the area around their cute little cocks. You're welcomed to come, too. Fanny and I do a mean waxing. Don't we?"

"Definitely. Hello, Mr. Darcy. I'm Lizzy's mom."

Elizabeth flung herself onto the bed and covered her face with her hands, mortified.

"So you're the one who sent the ransom note and racy photos?" Darcy asked.

"Me?" Mrs. Bennet exclaimed. "Certainly not."

"Not me!" Mary Bennet denied.

"What ransom note?" "Nude photos?" "I want to see them!" A bevy of women's voices overlapped each other.

"Mr. Darcy received photos of Lydia making love with Richard, but the face in the photos was doctored to be mine, instead of Lydia's," Elizabeth explained, with her hands covering her eyes. "They came with a ransom note demanding one million pounds for Richard's safe return."

Whistles were heard from the other end of the phone and, after some loud arguments, they heard Lydia begin to curse. "You shithead!" she exclaimed. This was followed by the sound of slapping. "You stole my love photos with Richard!"

"Yes, I did," Wickham cried. "I'm sorry, my gorgeous Lydia. Please just release me. Please. Urgh......"

"But why did you put *my* face on Lydia's body?" Elizabeth demanded.

"Yes, why? That was gross." Another smacking was heard before Lydia continued, "My body is so much better than Lizzy's. How could you degrade it by putting her face on MY body? Aunt, let me wax him."

"Urgh...No...Please...Urgh!" Wickham's shrieks persisted.

"Lydia is waxing Wicky's private parts now, very roughly," Mary stated, with the voice of a high ranking nun.

Amid sobs and pants, Wickham pleaded. "Please, I just wanted revenge on Lizzy for refusing to go out with me. I didn't mean to tarnish your lovely body, Lydia. Please, I don't want any more waxing!"

"You deserve it!" Darcy swore in a low voice before saying, more loudly, "Richard, should I send in the bodyguards?"

"Too...late." Richard's voice was weak. "Nearly all the hair on my body is gone. It hurts like hell. Lydia, love, you didn't say it would be such a torture."

Darcy shook his head and hung up the speaker phone with force. Then he looked down at Elizabeth, who was still lying on his bed, with her hands covering her eyes, breathing heavily.

He leaned down besides her and traced his knuckles along her arm.

She dropped her hands and gazed up at him.

As their eyes met, the misunderstanding seemed to fade away, and the atmosphere on the bed seemed to be charged with mega-kilowatts of electricity.

She raised her hand and caressed the red mark on his cheek. "I'm sorry that I hit you."

"I'm sorry that I said such foul things to you," he confessed shyly, and touched her hand to his face.

"You were just worried about your cousin." She smiled, licking her lips as she felt the heat from his body.

"And you have some very... uhm..." His dimples showed. "...interesting female relatives."

"Your cousin is interesting, too. I should probably explain that Jane and I haven't lived with my mother and younger sisters since I turned fifteen." She panted as she felt his hand drifting down to her waist. "We live with our father."

"So I don't need to worry about an invitation to a Brazilian waxing party?" He raised her hand and kissed the fingers.

"How about – " Gasping, she continued in a low voice. " – a slumber party, instead?"

He didn't need any more encouragement. His mouth descended on her sultry lips.

***

A year later, on a Friday evening after work, Elizabeth was pushed into a limo roughly by Mr. Darcy. The dividing panel was raised and a bottle of champagne was on ice.

"You can't kidnap me again!" Elizabeth exclaimed. Pushing him away, she sat opposite.

"Well, I have. And you won't be released..." He gazed at her with his deep brown eyes for a full minute. "...until you answer my question favourably."

She frowned. "What question?"

Moving like a panther, he knelt before her and grabbed her hand. "Will you marry me? My dearest, loveliest Elizabeth. Since our onerous start, I think I've redeemed myself. I've come to love, treasure and worship you during this past year. You're smart, honest and caring. You're simply awesome – the most wonderful woman that I've ever met. I want to have babies with you, to grow old with you, and to wake up with you, every day."

She could hear the tremor in his deep voice, sense the tightening of his body, feel the sweat from his hand. She was overcome with emotion. This handsome, hardworking, respectful man loved her so much that he was willing to overlook her unfortunate family relations and ask to spend the rest of his life with her. He could have any woman, with his wealth but he wanted her, and her alone.

She could only nod her head and press her lips to his.

The joy of having his proposal accepted put a wide grin on his face. He returned her kisses with vigour, angling her head in different ways as he sucked and kissed every corner of her lips. His hands were busy outlining the curves of her body, imprinting them on his mind.

She took charge, as well, pulling him up from his kneeling position and pressing him against the seat of the limo so that she could sit on his lap.

With frantic eagerness, he undid several buttons of her shirt, pushed her bra aside, and began to apply his hungry mouth to her nipples.

Gasping, she unbuckled his trousers, freed his thick cock, and stroked his hot, pulsing shaft with fluttering fingers.

Her actions broke his restraint. He suckled her nipples hard, making her moan out loud.

With one hand cradling his head, she pushed aside her underpants and positioned him at her entrance. He didn't need more prompting. His body had learned hers, over the past months. Grabbing her hips, he thrust upwards as she settled heavily onto him.

She felt his blazing rod stretching every muscle in her core, until he had pushed right to the hilt. Luckily, she was wet and ready. They stopped for air, breathing heavily against each other, before moving in a mad dash. Raising and lowering her body, she rode him ferociously. He was keen to help, as well, guiding her hips with his hands.

The sound of heavy breathing, and of slick muscles smacking together, echoed in the close confines of the back compartment of the limo.

The passionate storm escalated so quickly that they reached their climax within a few minutes. Darcy let out a loud shout, shivered and spilled his seed into the depths of her, while she squeezed her entire body tightly around him and bit his shoulder to contain the sensation.

Luckily, Mr. Darcy had planned to keep his captive in his house until she agreed to his proposal, that night. The tired but happy couple dragged themselves from the limo, into the garage and up to their love nest without meeting anyone.

His housekeeper and chauffer were no longer shocked by their employer's imperfect attire. They had seen it often enough, and did not raise their eyebrows anymore. This time, his trousers were wrinkled and buttoned incorrectly, and her shirt was not properly tucked into her skirt.

After the mistaken-identity kidnapping, Elizabeth's life was forever changed. To her delight (and his), she became the girlfriend – and then the wife – of Mr. William Darcy, one of the most eligible bachelors of England.

*What if Mr. Darcy wanted an heir?*

## Sacrifice

"Fuck you!" Elizabeth swore aloud at the tall man inches away from her.

"I believe I will," Darcy said quietly, before grabbing her by the waist and pulling her to his body. Lowering his head, he fitted his lips to hers, sucking hard, taking Elizabeth completely by surprise.

His passionate kiss quickly turned her to jelly. Her raised hands, which had originally aimed to strike his chest, ended up caressing his broad shoulders instead. When his tongue invaded her mouth with insistent thrusts, blood drained from her head and rioted through her body as aroused wetness pooled at her apex.

She couldn't breathe.

She couldn't think.

She leaned against the wall for support.

Then she heard a tearing sound, and felt his strong hands squeezing her butt. His hands were firm and hot against her cool, soft muscles.

Where had the coolness come from?

As he continued to kiss her senseless, she suddenly understood what the tearing sound was. He had ripped off her panties and was now fondling her bottom. Her naked bottom!

Her hands dug into his masculine back as she shivered under his ministrations.

Then his fingers traced a path through her curls, rubbing the wet folds, hard and fast.

She trembled, once, twice, again.

When he slipped two fingers into her entrance, she moaned out loud and scratched her nails over his back.

In and out, his fingers brought her to new heights. Coupled with his relentless kiss on her mouth, minutes by minutes, she was veering closer and closer to her climax.

Suddenly, he withdrew his fingers. She felt a tremendous loss, for a second. Then Darcy shoved his huge cock into her.

She didn't know when he had lowered his trousers. All she knew was that his thick shaft felt incredible as it invaded her tight muscles.

Inch by inch, he thrust inward, soon becoming impatient with the progress. Leaving her mouth for a moment, he groaned aloud before impaling her to the hilt with one mighty thrust.

Elizabeth gasped for air and bit into his shoulder.

After grinding his hips for a second, he began withdrawing and advancing. His thrusting was mad and wild. Like a machine, he pounded into her on and on, again and again. She was nailed and banged against the wall for what seemed like eternity. Their movements were so violent that a photo at the other end of the wall fell to the floor and broke into pieces.

In response, she was tore and bit at him -- his hair, his neck, his back – leaving love marks everywhere. Then, as suddenly as he had started screwing her, they both reached the edge and tumbled over. They trembled and convulsed together as his hot seed filled her core.

"Now, you're mine," Darcy murmured breathlessly. "Forever!"

"Dream on!" Elizabeth unwounded her legs from his waist, pushed him away, and made her wobbly way across the floor.

He let her move away, leaning himself against the wall, catching his breath. "You did say that this week was your optimal time...and that you're not taking the pill."

She froze, halfway through the act of bending down to pick up her torn underpants. "You did this deliberately!"

"You asked me to screw you," he reminded her as he tidied up his trousers and picked up her panties.

"If I get pregnant, I'll kill you." Holding out her hand, she waited with angry eyes for him to give her back the torn undergarment.

"You would rather that our little girl never has a chance to know her father?" He lifted the panties to his nose. After deeply inhaling their scent, he tucked the underpants into the breast pocket of his Armani suit.

"Give those back to me!" she yelped.

"We're not done yet." He walked closer and lifted her off her feet.

She struggled wildly, sending a vase to the floor. "Fuck you, Fitzwilliam Darcy! I will not be your baby machine."

Unable to hold onto her that way, he threw her over his shoulders and clasped her legs tightly against his chest to prevent her kicks. She pummelled his back, demanding to be put on the floor. Unfazed by her hitting, he smacked her bare bottom instead.

"Let me down!"

"Not until my sperms have had a chance to bury themselves deep inside your womb, again and again."

"Caveman! I will not have your baby."

He climbed the stairs quickly, as if she weighed nothing. "You don't have a choice. My daughter could already be inside you." He continued to spat her bottom as he walked, occasionally rubbing her wet folds, as well. Elizabeth's wild struggle was getting weaker. She moaned aloud when he put her down on the bed, tugged her hands above her head, and fastened them to the rails of the bed head with feathered handcuffs.

She tried to raise her legs and kick him, but he sat on them to prevent her movement. Then he bent forward and tore open her golden sundress, exposing the red lacy bra underneath. He pulled the bra down roughly, not bothering to take it off, then lowering his head to suckle her breasts.

She could no long resist, not with Darcy laving, licking and sucking at her nipples. When he shaped the rock hard peaks repetitively and then nipped at them, she screamed out in ecstasy. Her hands grabbed the headboard tightly as his tongue and lips devoured her cherries.

Just when she thought she would reach heaven, he stopped and moved down her body. Parting her legs widely, he buried his face in her apex, lapping at her pussy. She jerked and arched her body up and down, wildly uncontrolled, until she could stand it no more. A waterfall of sensation poured from her core, and she yelled as she reached an earth-shattering climax so intense that her mind became blank and her body went numb.

But the out-of-this-world experience was not yet finished. She felt him push one of her legs up to her upper body, exposing her at an unusual angle. She raised her sated gaze and saw that he had stripped off his clothes.

He was a beautiful six-foot-four specimen of strong muscles as he poised the hard length of his cock at her entrance. The sight was so magnificent that she began to tremble with fresh anticipation.

Without further delay, he drove his manhood into her hot wet entrance at an intense new angle, scorching skin that not been touched before, creating friction and pressure in muscles never used. His hands returned to her puckered, sensitive nipples. As he pounded into her wildly, madly, ardently, she bit her lip, thrusting her hips up to welcome his invading shaft.

She reached her second orgasm soon, shivering as she squeezed his cock tightly, until he, too, screamed out loud. Once again, his hot seed flooded her womb. Then he collapsed on top of her, his weight bearing down on her. He was still inside her as they both fell asleep.

Half an hour later, Darcy woke with a sense of deep satisfaction. And yet, when he moved to withdraw from Elizabeth's core, his arousal was stimulated again. As he unfastened the cuffs and turned her gently to lie on her stomach, she murmured in her sleep but did not protest.

With the help of the moonlight from the window, he admired her voluptuous curves. Her breasts were full, her nipples red, and the curve of her bottom looked delicious. The close examination raised his arousal further. Pulling her up slightly, he pushed her legs apart before positioning his thick cock and sliding into her warm, moist pussy.

"Ah!" Elizabeth cried out as she came awake. "What the fuck?" She grabbed the pillow and dug her fingers into the fabric.

"Yes, I'm fucking you." Darcy gritted his teeth as he squeezed her luscious breasts while pumping into her from the behind. His hips and body smacked onto her bottom, again and again.

She wriggled her buttocks, not sure whether she was trying to dislodge or welcome him. He held tight, pulling her nipples hard.

Her hands tore at the pillow as she received his hard pounding. "Bastard!"

"Our baby won't be a bastard. You're my woman." He rammed his huge cock deeper into her sex.

Her folds became swollen, her muscles sore, her butt sweaty. But Darcy was an insatiable beast, feasting on her sexual response. It was much, much later when, after giving her multiple orgasms, he finally reached his own climax, sending forth his essence to swamp her sex.

In this rough manner, Darcy locked Elizabeth up in his London townhouse for non-stop baby making sex for the entire week. Nine months later, little Jane Darcy was born at Pemberley, their first daughter after three sons. Mr. and Mrs. Darcy sent a hefty present to the psychic who had advised them that rough, non-stop sex for an entire week would cause them, finally, to conceive a baby girl.

In the years that followed, the couple had two more energetic daughters. But much of the furniture in their London residence needed replacing, after the rough weeks of conception ritual that led to that fine outcome.

Thank you Debra Anne and tJean

11903786R0012

Made in the USA
Lexington, KY
08 November 2011